A Note from the Editor

AIR MAIL
PAR AVION

I took my first "big trip" when I was thirteen years old. My mom and stepdad decided to take my sister and me to Mexico. And since my sis and I had never been out of the country before, we were pretty excited. We expected some scene from "The Love Boat" or "Fantasy Island": palm trees and white sand beaches, friendly locals in big sombreros, drinks with little umbrellas in them. I'll never forget the shock of crossing the border. We lived in southern California, but just by driving a few hours and stepping over an imaginary line, we entered a whole new world.

Gone were the bright-neon, sanitized McDonald's, the overcrowded, elevator-muzak malls, and the so-shiny-just-washed cars. Tijuana flooded me with its jumbled sights and sounds and smells. Thousands of tiny shops were packed to the gills with all kinds of crazy stuff, from pickles to piñatas and everything in between. The streets seemed hotter than in San Diego, which was just a few miles away, and they were certainly dustier and more crowded. Mixed with the unfamiliar scent of sewage were more pleasant odors: roasting corn

Going Places

True Tales from Young Travelers

Published by
Beyond Words Publishing, Inc.
20827 NW Cornell Road, Suite 500
Hillsboro, Oregon 97124
503-531-8700

ISBN: 1-58270-070-2

Cover and interior design by: Avery Maniscalco and Stephanie Leritz
Special thanks to: Kristin Hilton, Barbara Leese, Sarah Minnich, and Marianne Reid

Printed in the United States of America
Distributed to the book trade by Publishers Group West

Library of Congress Cataloging-in-Publication Data

McCann, Michelle Roehm, 1968–
Going places : true tales from young travelers / compiled by Michelle Roehm McCann ;
featuring 16 real kid adventurers.
p. cm.
Summary: Photographs accompany sixteen real-life stories of teenagers who describe
in their own words a journey that changed their lives.
ISBN 1-58270-070-2

1. Teenagers—Travel—United States—Juvenile literature. 2. Teenagers—United
States—Live skills guides—Juvenile literature. [1. Travel. 2. Coming of age. 3. Adventure
and adventurers.] I. Title.

HQ796 .M185 2003
305.235—dc21
2001058955

The corporate mission of Beyond Words Publishing, Inc:
Inspire to Integrity

Going Places

True Tales from Young Travelers

Compiled by
Michelle Roehm McCann

**BEYOND
WORDS**
Publishing
I N C

f Contents

on the cob, sweet sticky *churros y chocolate*, taco stands bursting with spicy smells. My mouth watered the whole day.

What I remember most clearly, however, are the kids. Of course I had seen homeless people before, but I'd never seen people begging. Especially not kids my own age. The minute we crossed the border, I was astonished to be in the constant company of at least one or two kids asking "*Chicle? Chicle?*" as they pushed their boxes of gum under our noses. The children didn't seem much younger than my sister and I, but they were considerably smaller. They walked barefoot on the hot sidewalks, their dark skin lightened by a fine layer of dust, their clothes hanging in rags from their too-skinny limbs.

Prior to this trip, I had spent a good part of my life whining and feeling sorry for myself. My mom and dad had gotten divorced when I was four, and I became a part of the dreaded "single-parent household." We were poor. I was horrified by the "free lunch" tickets I had to produce in the cafeteria every day in front of my friends. I was mortified by the obviously out of style hand-me-downs I had to wear, while my friends sported the coolest bell-bottoms money could buy. I wanted to sink into the linoleum every time my mom paid for our groceries with food stamps. I thought we were as poor as you could get and I hated it. Then I went to Tijuana.

It was pretty hard to continue feeling sorry for myself after Tijuana. I lived in a house (yeah, it was small, but it was a house). I got three meals a day and I never had to beg or sell anything except Girl Scout cookies. It began to sink in that I had more than one kid could ever possibly need, just because I lived across an imaginary line. How unfair was that?

I never knew how those kids felt about their lives. My Spanish was lousy back then. Did they know how spoiled most Americans were? Did they hate us all for how easy we had it? Maybe. What I did figure out is that life went on for those kids, in spite of their poverty. They didn't spend all their time hawking gum. They raced around the shops with their friends, they munched corn with their little brothers, and they played soccer in empty lots using plastic milk jugs for balls. They were kids, much like my sister and me.

It made me wonder: What's it like in other parts of the world? What do kids in China do? How do kids in the Amazon live? At age thirteen, I had officially been bitten by the travel bug.

In the many years since Tijuana, I've covered a good part of the globe. I've road-tripped through Europe, Asia, South America, and the United States. For each question I answer about other people in other parts of the world, a new question pops up, and I have to hit the road again to answer it.

Traveling is my passion. My passport is thicker than most people's wallets. I am still amazed that one experience, one border crossing when I was thirteen, caused this and changed my life forever.

The stories in this book were written by kids who have their own passions and took their own paths. Kids who, for one reason or another, found themselves on a journey that shifted their lives. From Alan Anderson's all-American RV road-trip with Dad, to Sarah Stillman's exploration of Cuba, their adventures opened up doors to a bigger world than they had even known existed. They were pushed to do things they'd never done before and to try things they'd never tried. They befriended people they were afraid of before. They faced their scariest demons and overcame their greatest obstacles. Going places changed these young writers forever.

I hope you find strength and inspiration in their stories, just as I have. I'm feeling that urge to load up my backpack right now! It's a big, exciting, wonderful world out there, and you'll never know it by sitting in front of the TV or hangin' at the mall. As these tales will tell, it's never too early to get going on your own adventure!

Bon Voyage!
Michelle

Chapter 1

Out on the Perimeter

U.S.A.

USA

From: Alan Anderson
Age: 17 years old
Where: U.S. Perimeter

AIR

DATE
STATE
U.S. POSTAGE
PB METER
≡ .00 ≡

A flock of golden September leaves fluttered to the ground while glimpses of green grass peeked through the leaves as a reminder of summer. School was starting like normal, but without me in it this year. In fact, everything that had been normal in my life was gone this year. My normal life began crumbling the year before, during a vacation in Montana, when a man pedaled out of the forest and told us his story.

A burly, redheaded man stopped his bike for a rest beneath a tree in Libby, Montana. My dad and I were sitting in the shade at a motel when we saw him.

"Where are you headed?" my dad asked, curious as usual.

"I'm finishing a bike ride around the perimeter of the United States," he answered. "I've been riding for two years."

That shocked us.

My dad asked the man, James, to dinner. That night, James told us stories from his trip. It sounded really interesting, but I thought to myself, "That's something I would never do." I liked my normal life.

My dad, on the other hand, thought the journey sounded incredible. I was sure he was just dreaming when he started talking about us doing something similar. But that dream became a reality one afternoon when I glanced out the window.

There it sat in the driveway: a 1977 Dodge camper. It was the kind of camper van you see retired people driving. Or families with lots of young children. Or surfers. We lived in Idaho . . . a long way from the beach. Looking out the window, I knew I was not related to that camper. My dad, however, came in beaming like he'd found a long-lost child. He must have felt sorry for it because years of neglect had left it tattered. But Dad could see the camper's potential underneath the layers of dirt, and its possibilities attracted him.

He devoted all his spare time to that thing, completely ripping out the insides and fixing everything that was broken. We hardly ever saw him anymore. Eventually the makeover neared completion. The outside looked the same (except that now it was clean), but the inside was unrecognizable. Dad had put in bunk beds and a sink, and everything, including the seats, was newly upholstered. The camper reminded me of a blue-and-white whale with an arched back and a short stubby snout. Only the wheels prevented it from swimming away in the ocean, as I wished it would.

My dad proposed taking several months and driving the camper around the perimeter of the United States. The plan was to head west to the Pacific Ocean, up the coast to the Canadian border, east across the top of the country, and south along the Atlantic Ocean. Once in Florida, it would be time to turn west, following the Gulf and the Mexican border until reaching the Pacific Ocean once again before heading home. Surprising everyone, even myself, I decided to go along.

As the trip drew closer, my head swirled with questions that couldn't be answered. I didn't know what to expect or how to prepare myself for stepping out into the unknown. I loved the big, white, colonial house I'd grown up in. How could I give it up to live in a camper that was smaller than my bedroom? What was I thinking? I hardly even recognized myself after the military-style haircut my dad gave me to begin the trip. Looking in the mirror, I felt like I had lost my identity.

When the time came, we filled the camper with supplies, hugged my sister, my brother, and my mom good-bye, then hit the road. As we pulled out of the driveway, my dad was looking forward to our adventure, and I was looking back at what I had known forever. Heading west, I watched everything familiar slide out of view.

I knew we were nearing the western perimeter when the vegetation turned a lush green and winds brought sounds of seagulls squawking and the smell of fish and salt in the air. That night we weaved up the Pacific coast, watching the sun slip away into ocean waves.

Our first stop on the journey was certainly an interesting one. Curtains of rain covered the land as we headed inland to Concrete, Washington. Atop a hill, we spotted a massive old school building that was being upgraded into what appeared to be a castle! It wore a crown of brand new turrets. We knocked on the door and were greeted with warm smiles and hugs by the owners, Jack and Phyllis. We had met them briefly the year before, while walking around Concrete on a vacation. It amazed me that now they welcomed us like family. We stayed in the castle for a week, helping Jack with renovations. It was nice to know someone else who was doing something just as strange as we were.

After Concrete, we headed east along the northern perimeter of the country. The camper battled its way up the pine-covered mountains and then coasted down into flat, treeless plains. Small farming towns dotted the empty highways every ten miles or so.

While driving through the monotonous fields of North Dakota, where skyscraper grain silos were the only forms that rose above the flat horizon, we pulled off into the town of Flaxton to get some lunch. The town looked abandoned except for one car parked at a tiny, old grocery store. Looking for food, we entered the store. The shelves seemed naked, stripped of almost everything. Was there a food shortage going on?

"Excuse me," my dad asked the lady at the cash register, "but where's all the food?"

"Today's our last day of business," she answered, a grim expression on her face.

The grocery store was the last business left; the next day, Flaxton would become a ghost town. We left the grocery store and walked along the crumbling sidewalks. Parched, overgrown lawns led up to houses with boarded-up windows. "For Sale" signs sprouted like weeds. The decaying town was creepy and reminded me of a cemetery. Like everyone else, we too left Flaxton. I wouldn't miss it.

Cold winter winds pushed us east to where a fire of color covered the New England trees in warm tones of red, yellow, and orange. When we reached Maine, we hit the Atlantic Ocean and began our descent along the eastern perimeter. Much to my disappointment, my dad made sure to avoid New York City and its swarming traffic. But on our circle around New York City, we had another wonderful accidental adventure. We stopped in the town of Monticello, New York, to stretch our legs a little, and while walking along the street, we were greeted with warm, friendly smiles by two black ladies.

"You going to church?" they asked us.

"Uh . . . no," my dad answered, not even realizing it was Sunday.

"Well, why don't you come along with us then? You'll love our church."

Of course my dad agreed. He was always looking for adventure. I wasn't so thrilled, however. I mean, the women were extremely friendly, but we didn't even know them.

When I entered the church, my fears were confirmed. Black faces surrounded me. My dad and I were the only white people there, and I felt nervous and out of place. Where I grew up, there weren't many black people. Until this day, I had never even spoken to a black person. What were we doing here? Some of the black churchgoers stared at me as if they thought I didn't belong there . . . or maybe they were just surprised; I couldn't tell. But when the church service began, no one paid any more attention to me. It was the most enthusiastic church crowd I had ever seen.

"Hallelujah!" and "Thank you, Jesus!" filled the air, while hands clapped, keeping time with the gospel music.

When the service ended, Mrs. Weathers, one of the women who'd invited us, asked us to stay at her house. We accepted. Arriving at the old house, Sister Weathers (as she liked to be called) introduced us to her husband, Brother Weathers. We stayed with them for a couple of days, while my dad fixed their car and gave Brother Weathers a haircut. The Weathers family didn't have a lot of material possessions, but they were so kind and loving that we immediately relaxed around them. I knew I could trust them, even though I hadn't known them very long.

One morning, as we ate breakfast together, Sister Weathers surprised me.

"Would it be all right if I touched your hair?" she asked politely.

"Sure," I said.

Reaching her dark, wrinkled hand out, she ran her fingers through my straight brown locks. "It's so soft," she said with amazement. "I never knew white people's hair was so soft." Sister Weathers had never touched a white person's hair until that moment.

When frost appeared on the camper's windows, we knew it was time to move on. The Weathers were so nice I didn't want to leave, but they sent their prayers with us. As we drove south out of New York State, the weather slowly improved, and as we neared Florida, I was wearing shorts again—in November.

As the number of palm trees increased, so did the hotels and tourist shops lining the coast. After many weeks on the road, we reached the most southern point in the United States—Key West, Florida. That meant we were finally heading home. We traveled through swamps where alligators waited like submerged logs, then followed the Gulf of Mexico toward the north and then west.

One evening in Louisiana we stopped in Morgan City for the night. As we headed out for our evening walk, Christmas lights blinked on like motionless fireflies outlining the houses and trees. It reminded me to work on convincing my dad to get back home for the holidays. Nothing sounded more depressing to me than Christmas in the camper.

At one well-lit home, we stood admiring the lights with the owner.

"Any interesting sights in town?" my dad asked, looking for adventure once again.

"Well . . ." said the man, scratching his chin, "there's Mr. Charlie. He's pretty interesting." That was enough to get my dad sidetracked from heading home.

The next morning, at sunrise, we set off to find the mysterious Mr. Charlie. We crossed the railroad tracks into the poor side of town and saw a sign pointing off to the right that read: "Mr. Charlie." We turned right and there he was.

Mr. Charlie sat at the edge of the riverbank, perched on thick, sturdy legs. It looked like a gray, two-story factory, built 100 feet up in the sky and connected to the ground by a long stairwell climbing one leg. The steel-mesh stairway was the only way inside, and my poor legs were exhausted by the time we reached the top. I could see the muddy bayou and the town of Morgan City way down below us.

Virgil Allen, the man in charge, gave us a tour of Mr. Charlie. We walked through corridors of bedrooms, a large kitchen, and a lounge area that took up two floors. Mr. Charlie was retired but had been the first offshore oilrig ever built. It now served as a museum and training station for roustabouts, the new workers on oilrigs. As we were getting ready to leave, my dad surprised me.

"Is there any way we could stay here on Mr. Charlie for a while?" he asked, full of his usual eager enthusiasm.

"You mean work as roustabouts?" asked Virgil. He sounded as shocked as I felt.

"Sure. Why not?"

And that was that. Later that day, Dad and I became official roustabouts-in-training. I guessed we wouldn't be home for Christmas after all.

We got our own room, plus all our meals prepared by the on-board cook. We had to work on a few projects, but most of the time, we were left to explore Morgan City. Virgil's son and I became friends, and the whole Allen clan embraced us as a part of their family. We even celebrated Christmas with them. My first Christmas away from home will hopefully be my last. Being away from the rest of my family during the holidays made me realize how much I really missed them.

The story of our journey spread around Morgan City, and before long, the local newspaper wanted to do an article about us. They took our picture and did an interview, and when the paper came out, I couldn't believe my eyes—we were on the front page! I was pretty thrilled to be famous in that small town. So many good things happened to us in Morgan City that it was hard to leave. But after a month of living as roustabouts, we decided to leave Mr. Charlie and head back to our real home.

The swamps disappeared along with the dense vegetation as we drove through the arid southwest. Stunted junipers clung to rocky outcroppings and the mountains radiated a reddish glow. We climbed up California and crossed the Sierra Nevada Mountains in our trusty little camper. We were getting so close now; home was like a magnet pulling us back.

When the camper pulled into our driveway, it was hard to believe that just four months (and 13,507 miles!) earlier I had been standing in that very place. It felt like a lifetime had gone by. I had been dreaming about this moment for many nights—from inside the camper, the castle, the ghost town, atop Mr. Charlie, and even at the home of the Weathers family. Whenever I felt alone (which happened, even among new friends), I turned to my memories of home for comfort.

Swinging open the camper door, I breathed in the cold, fresh air of February. It was the end of one season, and the start of another; spring would be here soon. I ran to my front door and knocked hard. It opened and out came my mom. She hugged me in her arms, but my brother and sister just stared, as if I were a stranger. Maybe they had thought we'd never return. But return we had. There was a fire burning in the fireplace, and its warmth surrounded me. I was finally home where I belonged.

Looking back, I see that our journey around the perimeter of the United States was more difficult and more wonderful than I had ever expected. Setting out, I never thought I would feel so alone or vulnerable, but I survived. I also never thought we'd make so many good friends. I often wonder, will I ever see those people again, or will they just drift away into my memory? Will I ever visit those places again? I don't know the answers, but I do know that each little piece of America affected me. Each person and each place. Now all those pieces are like a quilt, stitched together inside me.

The Abernathy Boys

b.1900 and b.1904 ✦ From Oklahoma to New York

The folks of Cleveland, Ohio, could barely keep their eyeballs from popping out of their heads. They crowded six deep along the road, trying to get a peek at the new arrivals. Why all the fuss? It wasn't just to check out the motor car, which itself was an oddity during the horse-and-buggy days. They were staring so hard because underneath the dusty goggles and leather driving helmets were two boys! Ten-year-old Bud and his six-year-old brother Temple were driving from New York back home to Oklahoma . . . by themselves! (Obviously, this was before the days of licenses and car insurance.)

The Abernathy boys, as they were called, must have inherited their adventurous spirits from their father. Jack "Catch 'em Alive" Abernathy had raised Bud and Temple on his own after their mother died. Their father was famous for catching wolves on horseback, leaping onto their backs and wrestling them to the ground with his bare hands. On a visit to Oklahoma, President Theodore Roosevelt was so impressed with Jack's stunt that he gave him a job as a U.S. Marshal (a fancy kind of sheriff). With a wolf wrestler for a dad, it was pretty much "anything goes" for the boys.

When they were just nine and five, Bud and Temple dreamed up their first adventure: to ride horses from Oklahoma to Santa Fe, New Mexico, and back again. They had no reason for the trip; they wanted to go just for the fun of it. Even though Temple was so small he had to mount his horse from a porch, their father thought it was a great idea. The Abernathy boys made it to Santa Fe and back with no problems, but shortly after their return Jack received a note from a band of cattle rustlers he had been after for months. The thieves had tailed Bud and Temple on their return to Oklahoma with the intention of doing them harm. Luckily they changed their minds:

> [We] don't like one hair on your head, but [we] do like the stuff that is in these kids. We shadowed them through the worst part of New Mexico to see that they were not harmed by sheepherders, mean men, or animals.

The next year, the Abernathy boys came up with an even wilder plan. They wanted to ride from Oklahoma to New York City to meet the new president, William Howard Taft, and their father's buddy, former president Theodore Roosevelt. Once in the Big Apple, they planned to ditch their horses and return home in a new-fangled automobile. Once again, their father gave them an enthusiastic thumbs-up.

On the two-month ride east, Bud and Temple were greeted by enthusiastic crowds and marching bands in cities like St. Louis, Cincinnati, Columbus, and Baltimore, where they charmed local reporters. They were hosted by such celebrities of the day as Quanah Parker, last of the Comanche war chiefs, and the Wright Brothers, pioneer aviators. And once they hit the East Coast, they did, in fact, get to meet their presidents. Taft visited with them at the White House and Roosevelt met them in New York. The Abernathy boys had become bona fide national heroes.

While their horses took a train back to Oklahoma, Bud and Temple bought themselves a Brush Runabout, one of the first cars ever built, for $485. To start the engine, they had to get out and crank a handle on the front of the car. After one afternoon of driving lessons from the car salesman, roaring up and down Broadway in New York City, they headed for home. If they drew crowds on their horseback trip, just imagine the hordes that showed up to gawk at them in their car.

You might imagine that it would be easier to drive across the country than to ride a horse, but keep in mind that cars were still fairly new, and there weren't that many in existence. That meant few paved roads and no highways. No fast food. No gas stations. No tow trucks. The boys had to drive mostly on rutted dirt and grass-covered roads. They had to get gas and food at whatever small-town stores they could find. And if the car broke down (which was common), they either had to find someone to fix it (unlikely) or fix it themselves.

But the boys did make it home. By the time they pulled up to their ranch in Cross Roads, Oklahoma, the Abernathy boys had set a cross-country driving record—2,512 miles in 23 days—even though Temple had to sit on the very edge of the seat and lean against the steering wheel to reach the driving pedals. All in all, the boys had traveled more than 5,000 miles on their journey . . . all by themselves.

So, the next time your folks say you're too young to borrow the car, why not tell them the story of the amazing Abernathy boys?

Chapter 2

My Great Thanksgiving Journey

From: Miles Pierson-Brown
Age: 12 years old
Where: North Carolina

Every other year at Thanksgiving, I travel all the way across the country to North Carolina to visit my auntie, Dr. Maya Angelou, for a week. She throws the best Thanksgiving party in the world. For those of you who don't recognize the name, my auntie is a famous poet and writer. At her Thanksgiving event, I've met many famous, talented people: Malcolm X's widow, Dr. Betty Shabazz; Oprah Winfrey; musicians Ashford and Simpson; and many others. But more than the celebrity guest list, I love Auntie Maya's party because *everyone* gets to be creative and show their stuff. Even me.

North Carolina in November is pretty similar to Oakland, California, where I live. The temperature is about 60 degrees, it's pretty sunny, and the trees have lost most of their leaves. One thing I've noticed about North Carolina that's different than California is that smoking is still allowed in public buildings. North Carolina is a "tobacco state"; tobacco is a very important crop, and lots of cigarettes are made there. And lots of people in North Carolina smoke, especially at the airport.

My family, along with four or five other families, stays at my auntie's guest house. It's a big, white house, but it's also very cozy and comfortable. It has a huge yard and lots of trees. There's a giant dining room table where we eat, and a TV room with a big-screen TV where we watch movies and play video games. Downstairs there's my auntie's office, which is converted into a huge play area for the kids during our Thanksgiving visit. My sister and the other girls her age sleep together in a big room that we call the "ballroom." It looks like a dormitory with all the beds lined up together.

Most of the kids who come to the party are my sister's age, that is, a few years older than me. Sometimes they leave me out of what they're doing, so I've made my own friends there. I've learned that I can go all the way across the country and make new friends in a week, then keep them as friends as the years go by. My North Carolina friends and I go to the movies and to the mall. We love going to a certain bowling alley that is the *best*! It's got neon lighting and the shoes and bowling balls light up in the dark! I'm a pretty good bowler—I usually get one of the highest scores.

Aside from bowling and hanging out, there are two big events during the week at my auntie's: Thanksgiving Dinner and Presentation Night.

For Thanksgiving dinner, the biggest tent I've ever seen is set up in my auntie's backyard. It has a big front room where music plays and people dance, then a hallway leads to an even bigger room where we eat dinner. About a hundred people come to celebrate, so there are lots and lots of round tables decorated for Thanksgiving by my Aunties Rosa and Stephanie. All of us kids get to sit together. When it is time to eat, my Uncle Guy says a beautiful grace, thanking all of us for being there and sharing our love together. Then the kids race to the buffet table first! We load our plates up with roast beef, ham, turkey, stuffing, mashed potatoes, sweet potatoes, vegetables, rolls, and gravy. The food is cooked by lots of the men who are at the dinner, with my Auntie Maya helping out. And there are about a million pies for dessert.

A couple of nights later is Presentation Night. Everyone (kids and adults) spends the week practicing for this big event. Different groups of people perform poetry, skits, songs, dances, and music. My sister and her friends always do a dance they choreograph themselves. Last year they danced to "What's Going On?" and everyone loved it. My dad's a great singer and he sang "People Get Ready" with his friends Calvin and Tim. They really harmonized. My mom recited a poem. Some of the presentations are serious and some are hysterical, but it's all fun to watch.

Last year, my cousin Elliot and I did the lighting and sound for the show. We were in charge of moving equipment around for each new performances and for playing music on a CD player during the transitions between acts. Next time, maybe I'll get up on stage and perform myself. (I play the saxophone, and when I did my African dance performances at school, everyone told me I was really good.)

These Thanksgiving trips mean a lot to me because I have gotten to know so many interesting people. They are role models for me. My Auntie Maya inspires me to work hard and to never give up my dreams. She has gone through a lot in her life but she has never given up. And look at her now: she is famous and loved all over the world. My family and friends at the Thanksgiving party have also taught me many things. I've learned that it's not just the famous people who have talents; they're just better known for theirs. Everyone has creativity in them. Even me!

I have lots of special memories from my Thanksgiving journeys, and every other year I look forward to making more. Who knows? Next year I might even read this essay at Presentation Night.

Chapter 3

Strudel

From: Whitney Quon
Age: 18 years old
Where: Europe

Just one year ago, I was incapable of doing anything on my own. At school I always begged someone to go with me the twenty feet to the bathroom, in case someone dared to make fun of me as I walked there alone. At lunch, I asked friends to accompany me through the lunch line, and if they said no, I just skipped lunch. I was a wimp. I was convinced that I was incapable of being by myself or making new friends. Basically, I thought I was a pathetic excuse for a human being.

This was a very hard way to live. I knew that I needed a change, but I didn't know what to do.

The opportunity came to me in the summer after my junior year, disguised as a sixteen-day musical trip through Europe as part of a band and choir representing the state of Oregon. I was intrigued by the idea. I would get to travel all around seven magnificent countries . . . but with 285 *strangers*.

My journey began with three days of rehearsal at Lewis & Clark College, where we practiced for our European performances and got to know the other musicians we'd be traveling and playing with. I arrived on campus and realized, "I don't know a single person here and I have to spend sixteen days with these people." My stomach churned, tears came to my eyes, and all I could think about was how much I already wanted to go home. And I hadn't even left Oregon.

Throughout the first rehearsal and opening meeting I visualized eating every meal by myself. I would bring a book and read while I ate as fast as I could. That way I wouldn't evoke anyone's sympathy and force them to join me, when I was sure no one would want to. Once we got to Europe, I would sit by myself, look at the scenery, and enjoy the peaceful solitude. I was petrified.

As I left the rehearsal and walked out towards that first dreaded meal, I felt tears coming again. I felt so alone. But then I heard something that surprised me:

"Whitney! How was choir rehearsal?" It was Liz, an oboe player I had met while signing in. "Can I eat with you?"

I couldn't believe what I was hearing. She wanted to eat with me. Maybe she even wanted to be my friend. A huge smile burst onto my face.

"Sure," I said, and I thought: "Maybe this won't be so bad after all."

Over the next few days at the college, I made even more friends. I was getting more confident that I wouldn't be abandoned at mealtimes. But in the back of my mind, I still feared that I would be deserted with nothing to do and nowhere to go. I presumed that all my new "friends" were just putting up with me because they felt sorry for me. As soon as we got to Europe, I was sure they'd forget about me and leave me in my room, alone, without looking back.

When the three days of rehearsal ended, I spent one last night at home with my family and confessed my fears to my mother.

"Whitney, you are just being silly. You will be fine. Stop worrying."

It was so easy for her to say. But scenarios kept flashing through my mind. I'd be stuck alone in some hotel room in France, crying because I had no one to talk to. And I'd get so homesick I wouldn't want to do anything. These images made me shudder. I wanted to have fun. I knew this was the chance of a lifetime. But what if . . .

The time came for me to say good-bye to my parents for sixteen long days. I shook with fear, but I knew I had to do it.

It was a test. Tears flowed freely from my eyes. I knew I had to get on the plane and get away.

"Mom, don't make me go," I pleaded, choking back more tears. "I can't do this. I can't."

"Whitney, you can and you will," she said, looking me right in the eyes. "I love you very much, but you have to do this. You are going to have such a wonderful time that you won't even think about us. I promise."

I tried not to look back as I began boarding the plane. I felt someone give me a comforting pat on the back. It was Kristen, another oboe player I had met during rehearsals.

"Wanna switch seats when we get on the plane?" she asked, smiling. "That way we can sit together on the flight."

I turned and waved one last time to my parents, then climbed on board, feeling a little better. I sat in my seat and saw Kristen sit two rows ahead of me. She turned around and gave me a huge smile.

"Whitney! Ask the girl next to you if she wants to change seats."

The girl next to me was already smiling and getting up. Kristen plopped down next to me, barely able to contain her excitement.

"Yay! I get to sit by you for the first leg of the flight."

I was astonished. She wanted to be my friend as much as I wanted to be hers. It wasn't just an act. Joy filled me up, and I started looking forward to the rest of the trip.

Once we were in the air, Liz came over to chat.

"How about the three of us room together in London?" she asked.

"That would be so great!" exclaimed Kristen.

They both looked at me expectantly.

"Awesome!"

I could barely contain myself. I couldn't stop smiling.

Everything was going to go well. I had two friends to help me through.

That first night of the trip, our chaperones thought we were crazy. We made so much noise talking and laughing that everyone could hear us up and down the hall. But that just made us laugh harder. None of us wanted to sleep that night; we were having so much fun getting to know one another. Finally we realized that it was just the first night and we would be together for the whole trip.

Those sixteen days changed my life. Each day I woke up to a new adventure. But I wasn't alone. When I performed as part of the choir at St. Mark's in Venice, Liz and Kristen came to watch. When Liz wanted to find a stein (a German drinking mug) for her boyfriend, we went along and offered our opinions. We ate lunch at cute French cafes. We watched in awe as the fog cleared and the Swiss Alps appeared. We walked silently through the Dachau concentration camp in respect for the people who had died there.

The times that I spent with Liz and Kristen were wonderful, but as the trip went on, I found time for myself. One afternoon in Austria, my friends wanted to take a nap.

Instead, I decided to explore Seefeld, the town we were staying in, to see what it had to offer. Each little shop had a very different flavor. Some were touristy shops with magnets and trinkets I had seen many times before. Others offered handmade treasures that helped me lighten my wallet considerably. The smells wafting from a bakery lured me in for a little taste of Austrian pastries. As I devoured one fabulous piece of strudel, I realized that before this trip I never would have explored some strange, foreign town by myself, not even a little place like Seefeld. Even though I had new friends, I wasn't afraid to be on my own anymore.

I found myself in those sixteen days. I became someone capable of surviving on my own. All too soon it was time to go home, even though I desperately wanted to stay in that magical place with all the wonderful people I had met and come to love.

When the day came, I walked off the plane and found my parents. I was overjoyed to see them. I had missed them a lot. But after the initial excitement I found myself longing to find Liz and Kristen. They had become a new family to me over those sixteen days. It was as painful to leave them as it had been to leave my parents what seemed like such a long time ago. We hugged and cried and promised that we would see each other again. This left me truly alone in the world to see if I could remain the person I had become.

Three months later, on a trip to San Francisco, my mom asked me to go get breakfast. I grabbed my purse and headed out the door alone without hesitation. The smell of the cool morning air made me smile, and the smells of a nearby bakery made me hungry. Strudel was their specialty.

Rosie Swale

b. 1947 — ✦ From Switzerland to just about everywhere

Who could imagine that a baby who was abandoned at a post office would grow up to become one of the greatest adventurers of all time? That's Rosie Swale for you: from Little Orphan Annie to Indiana Jones! And we're not talking posh airplane trips or luxury cruises, either. Rosie *walked* to India on her bare feet, rode halfway down South America on horseback, jogged through the Sahara Desert, trekked across Iceland, and sailed around the world. When the dictionary-makers defined the word "globe-trotter," they were probably thinking of Rosie.

It seems that she was born wearing traveling shoes. Soon after Rosie's birth, her mother died and the baby was left on the doorstep of a post office in Switzerland. Authorities found her grandmother in Ireland, who fetched Rosie back "home." Growing up in the 1950s, Rosie rarely went to school. Gramma Swale wasn't a big believer in formal education; she thought her grand-daughter would learn more from real life and from traveling. Instead of sending Rosie to class, she taught her to read and took her on trips.

When Rosie was a teenager, she set off on her own. First she went to London, where she worked as a typist and a model. Soon, however, she was itching for a bigger

adventure. One morning, instead of going to their boring jobs, Rosie and a girlfriend decided to go to India!
Unlike today, it was rare for young women to travel on
their own back in the early 1960s. But that didn't stop
them. The girls traveled more than 16,000 miles—by
car, bus, train, camel, and on foot—through Europe,
Turkey, and Iran to India, and then through Scandinavia
and Russia on their way back.

Rosie was such a hardy gal that when she lost her
only pair of shoes in Iran, she decided to travel the
remaining 2,000 miles to India barefoot! When she finally reached the desert, her feet began to burn on the
scorching sand. Did she break down and buy a pair of
flip-flops? Of course not! Rugged Rosie just tore her
handkerchief in two, wrapped up her roasting feet, and
walked on.

Once bitten by the travel bug, Rosie never stopped
moving. In the 1970s, she got married, had a daughter,
and immediately set sail with her family (including two
cats!) on a 30-foot catamaran. Together they sailed
around the world. Rosie even gave birth to her son out
in the middle of the ocean!

In 1983 Rosie sailed by herself in a small 17-foot
boat from England to America to raise awareness and
money for cancer treatment (her best friend had died
from cancer). Even though she nearly ran out of food
and water, even though she nearly lost her life several
times when she was swept overboard, and even though
she had to lash herself to the deck during one particu-

larly nasty storm, Rosie toughed it out and finished her record-breaking 4,800-mile solo voyage in seventy days.

Still not enough adventures for you? Well, the next year Rosie was the first person to ride a horse 3,000 miles down the entire length of Chile to Cape Horn. In the 1990s she journeyed to Libya just as the Gulf War was starting and had to escape through North Africa. Still not enough? Okay . . . she also jogged from the Black Sea to Transylvania to raise money for Romanian orphans. She even trekked across Iceland! And just when you think Rosie ought to be retiring, she goes and runs 150 miles across Africa in 130 degree heat for the Sahara Marathon. She was fifty-three years old!

Rosie is still traveling the world, writing books, speaking about her adventures, and breaking new records. She is living proof that you're never too young—or too old—to have adventures.

Chapter 4

Two Faces of India

From: Anarghya Vardhana
Age: 13 years old
Where: India

Staying in the same atmosphere for years with no change can be suffocating. To prevent that suffocation, my parents, my sister, and I make an annual trip to India, where my parents are originally from. India is a beautiful and enchanting country. A trip to that captivating place every year means that my sister and I soak in the ancient and rich Indian culture and get out of the rigmarole of daily material life; however, more than anything, the visit to India is meant to be a reunion with family members and a trip down the nostalgic memory lane.

 During the (dull, boring, dreary, mind-numbing . . . need I go on?) 26-hour airplane ride (with two-hour breaks at three different airports!), I usually gripe and whine about the boredom, the tasteless food, how hot or cold I am, how long the flight takes, and a variety of other ludicrous things. I never really considered that my parents spend thousands of dollars every year so that I can have this unique experience. Instead, I was always focused on my own self. But my so-called tradition of griping changed on our 1999 trip. That was when I first noticed the "two faces" of India and realized how lucky I was.

It was June 12, 1999. We had just arrived at the Portland Airport and were awaiting our flight to India. As we tried to kill time, this was the crazy scene:

1. My sister was trying to drive me insane (as usual);
2. My mother was tense, worrying that we'd forgotten to pack something (as usual);
3. My father was calm and in the mood for joking and/or eating (as usual); and
4. I was really getting annoyed with my sister (as usual, and much to her delight).

Miraculously, despite all those circumstances, we managed to get on the plane and set off for India. After so many stops, I thought we'd never get there—San Francisco, Cincinnati, Frankfurt, Bombay, and finally our destination: the Mangalore airport, at the southwestern tip of India.

Stepping off the plane, a hot humid blast of air hit me like a wall! My skin tingled—I was on Indian soil! I wanted to race out of the airport and find my grandparents, but unfortunately I was weighed down with tons of luggage. When we eventually got our luggage on a cart and out of the airport, I craned my neck from side to side trying to locate my *Ajja* and *Ajji* (grandfather and grandmother) in the sea of people.

As I strode quickly through the crowd, I suddenly cringed as a filthy child brushed past me, reaching a hand out for money. The kid was a puny, malnourished seven- or eight-year-old, and I could see his ribs through his tattered clothing. "Yew!" I thought. "That kid must not have showered in a month. He smells putrid." I lurched away from the beggar and continued searching for my grandparents.

After much craning of my poor sore neck, I spotted them across the crowd. My grandfather still had his noble look, even though he was sixty. His hair was pure white and he had a slight mustache. Having been a lawyer for the past thirty-five years, he looked stern. But once you got to know him, he was a lot of fun. My grandmother was by his side, all smiles. I loved my grandmother; she had an air of superiority around other people, but at the same time she made them feel comfortable enough to tell her all their problems. As always, she was dressed in a dazzling silk *sari* and wore earrings with seven diamonds each! Her delicate nose had a diamond stud. (It is a custom in India for women to pierce their noses. Of course, *I'll* never do that—I'm scared to get shots at the doctor!) I pushed past the crowd and threw myself on my Ajja and Ajji.

After the hugs, kisses, and tears, we sped off in my grandfather's luxuriously air-conditioned car. I leaned back against

the plush satin seats and relaxed. The horrible airplane trip
was over, and the dirty beggar was gone from my mind; I
could peacefully enjoy my vacation! But just as I was starting
to get into a mellow state of mind, we drove past a slum.
Reality hit me again. I stared at the tent city made out of
plastic bags, cardboard, and other garbage. From the cool
interior of the car, I could see naked children chasing a
ragged puppy, older kids begging, and their haggard-looking
mothers stirring pots over open fires. And what was I thinking, looking at this sad scene? "Disgusting! How can they live
in such unhygienic conditions? Good thing they can't get to
me." I felt safe in the car. "Whew!"

Arriving at my grandfather's mansion, I was ready for two
months of relaxation. Our family in India is a joint family,
meaning that my grandpa, grandma, great-uncle, great-aunt,
uncle, aunt, and three cousins (plus five dogs, ten cows, and
various other animals) all live together as one big happy family. In my opinion, this is what makes India the best place in
the world! Along with the family are plenty of servants who
seemed to fulfill our every wish. They cleaned up any messes
we made, so we didn't have to worry about putting things
away. Cooks prepared all the meals, which were delicious,
and I never had to wash a dish (my least favorite chore back
home). The servants were also our personal guides if we
ever wanted to tour my grandfather's 40-acre plantation. We
even had a driver to take us around in any of the three air-
conditioned cars.

My Ajja's house is also incredibly beautiful, with its sleek
marble floors, dark mahogany furniture, and fine works of
art. Back home in the U.S., my dad is no Bill Gates! We are

an ordinary middle-class family, living in an ordinary house,
in an ordinary neighborhood.
Despite being so ordinary, my
sister and I adapted to the
ultra-luxury and royal lifestyle
of my grandfather's house
pretty quickly! We whiled away

our summer playing, sleeping, and eating (and only occasionally whining).

But for some reason, I wasn't totally content. I had every
comfort I could hope for but still felt incomplete. Then it
started to dawn on me: aside from my family, friends of my
grandparents, and the servants, we hadn't seen anyone else
for a whole month. In fact, in all my visits to India, I had
never really had a chance to see the regular people of the
country. By "regular people," I mean the woman who sold
flowers by the side of the road, the old man who rode his
bicycle from house to house delivering milk, the next-door
neighbor who worked as a bank clerk.

In case you couldn't tell from the house and servants, my
grandfather and his family are pretty wealthy and mostly
associate with other wealthy Indians. I found myself thinking
about the children I'd seen at the airport and on the drive to
my grandparents' house. Children who looked like me but
had such different lives. I wondered, "What is it like for other
Indian families? Regular Indians? And what about the poor
people?" No matter what else I did, I couldn't get these
questions off my mind.

So when my uncle came up with the idea of visiting

Mysore Palace, I jumped at the chance. Mysore is an ancient city of temples, forts, and palaces located about twelve hours from my grandfather's house. It is the center of culture and learning in southern India, so I knew that the palace would be a popular destination. It would be teeming with Indian tourists, merchants, and even beggars—the other face of India I was longing to see. Feeling stifled by my pampered, languishing lifestyle, I was excited by the prospect of an adventure. It would also be an awesome way to see how my great-great-great (I have no idea how many "greats") grandfather lived. He was the royal mathematician at Mysore Palace!

The next morning I couldn't wait to start the scenic twelve-hour drive to Mysore. My fascination with the scenery wore off quickly, however, and my sister and I were back to our regular routine: arguing and bugging our parents. Fortunately the drive didn't last forever and we cruised into the bustling city around 10 P.M. I could barely fall asleep that night, I was so excited. "Tomorrow I'll be part of the action. I'll be one of the regular people walking the streets of Mysore!"

The next morning, as soon as I stepped out of the hotel into the sunlight, traffic, and action of India, my heart started beating faster. Cars whizzed past me, people honked and yelled, vendors bellowed about their wares, dogs chased each other yipping, cowbells jingled, people yelled for taxis, and a thousand other things were happening all around me. Although I might look like a typical Indian from the outside, inside I'm totally American! Like any American would be, I was overwhelmed by the hustle and bustle of this Indian city but fascinated, too. It was all part of the adventure.

After the initial shock of seeing the entire hullabaloo, my family and I weaved down the road, dodging people, cars, carts, and animals, and soon found ourselves in front of the famous Mysore Palace. When my uncle said the word "palace" the day before, I imagined elegance, wealth, gold, silver, and jewels. Don't get me wrong: the palace was beautiful. But the area around it shocked me, to say the least. The palace was surrounded with dozens of old men who were missing arms or legs, children who had no eyes, and women with large, hideous growths on their faces. All of them were trying their best to make money for their decaying families. The scene hit me like a steamroller. I felt like I wanted to cry.

"Why has this never bothered me before?" I thought. I guess I had always categorized these people as "poor people" and nothing more. As soon as I stopped seeing them, I forgot about them. "What is so special about today," I wondered, "for me to feel so sorry for them?" Sure, I had seen poor people before—back home in America and even in India—but nothing prepared me for this. Before, I was always in a car or watching them on the news. I was at a safe distance, removed from their suffering. But at Mysore Palace, for the first time, I was up close and personal with the other side of India. I could see and hear and feel these people's pain. It surrounded me.

In earlier years, I didn't see the poor people as anything like me ... I almost felt like they were a different species. But now, as I stared, I realized that they were just people. People like my family and me. I was also amazed at how they tried to bring out the silver lining in their difficult lives. Some used their talents to carve beautiful statues out of twigs and rocks from the road. Others made instruments and played melodious tunes. The children also had lives beyond the ones we saw on the streets. Some went to the railway station to learn how to read and write by studying newspapers thrown away by passengers. And when they weren't begging or working to get food, the children still found time to play with their friends—just like kids in America. I could finally see that despite their hardships, the poor people of India were

not so different from me after all.

In those hours that we toured the grounds, something changed in me forever. The contrast between the rich, magnificent palace and the poverty-stricken people around it jumped out at me like a crow amongst a flock of parrots. All my life I had cried, whined, and pouted over trivial things: not getting the clothes I wanted, having to eat certain foods, doing homework on sunny days—such unimportant details. The poor people in India were overjoyed just to get a morsel of food. They scavenged through garbage cans to find anything edible, even a banana peel. What in the world did I have to complain about?

During my previous visits to India, I had been critical of the poor people and even considered them below me, as if their poverty was their fault. In India, the Hindu religion puts everyone into four major castes, or classes: *Brahmins* (scholars and priests), *Kshatriyas* (warriors), *Vaishyas* (farmers and merchants), and *Shudras* (laborers and servants). Social outcasts, like beggars, are considered to be beyond the caste system. They are referred to as *Untouchables* and are not to be associated with or even touched by Brahmins (like me), who are the highest caste. Back in America, I always tried to be fair to all people, no matter what their race, color, or religion was. But in India, I had unknowingly fallen into my caste role! After visiting Mysore Palace, however, I realized that the "untouchables" are really no different from me. They are just people who were dealt bad cards in the poker game of life.

Now that I'm back home, I can't say that I'm a total Mother Teresa or anything. But I have changed. One thing I started doing right away, as soon as I got back to my grandfather's house, was to give my *dakshina* to the poor. A dakshina is a pretty good amount of money you receive at Indian functions, kind of like a goody bag just for attending. Earlier, I had spent my dakshina on bubble-gum, sweets, and other junk. But after my experience at Mysore Palace, I realized it was more important for little kids to get their food than for my spoiled teeth to rot. Three years later, I still give away my dakshina every year when I go to India.

But the major change in my life is that I will never see India in quite the same way again. I can't ignore or hide from India's other face. That evening when we returned from Mysore Palace, visions of limbless men and blind children flashed through my mind again and again. They still do, even today, especially whenever I start whining about something stupid.

Chapter 5

You Can't Judge a Book by Its Cover . . . or a Country Either

From: Sophie Glover
Age: 13 years old
Where: Croatia

Every year, millions of American kids move, leaving behind their homes, friends, schools . . . everything that's familiar to them. In fact, the average American family moves once every five years! So the odds are good that each of us will move two or three times before we even graduate from high school! Although it may be something most of us go through as we're growing up—having to make new friends, learning our way around a new town and a new school—it's also different for each of us. Here's my story.

The summer before seventh grade, I was on vacation with my family in New Mexico. We were climbing in ancient Pueblo Indian villages, horseback riding, and white-water rafting. I was having a great time and thinking no further ahead than the *NSYNC concert I was going to with my best friends the next week. Then the day before we were supposed to go home to Maryland, my parents dropped a bombshell. Oh, by the way, Dad's company is moving him—and the rest of us—overseas! In just a few months! To Zagreb, Croatia!

Okay, admit it—you probably have no idea where Croatia is, right? Neither did I. My parents told me that it was in the Balkans . . . part of what used to be Yugoslavia . . . just east of Italy . . . in Europe. Yeah, it didn't mean a whole lot to me, either.

Not surprisingly, I was shocked and angry. I didn't want to leave my friends behind! The international school I'd be going to in Croatia was tiny—not to mention in Croatia. Would I ever find anyone to hang out with? And we'd be in Croatia for two years! Would my friends at home remember me when I got back? And what about all the dances, slumber parties, and other fun stuff I'd miss out on? My parents tried to tell me, "This is going be a great experience for our family. And for you, too. Just wait and see." I was skeptical, to say the least.

When school started in September, I told all my friends we were going to Croatia next month. Everyone had the same questions: Where is that? Is it safe? Isn't there a war going on there? What language do they speak? How do you

spell it—Kroatia, Croasia, Kroasia? Of course, no one had
ever been there. And I sure didn't have any answers.

Then one day my Social Studies teacher showed us
Croatia on a map of Europe. Yep, there it was, a green boom-
erang sandwiched between Slovenia and Bosnia-Herzegovina.
How did we ever miss it? My teacher explained about the
war Croatia fought in the 1990s to win independence from
communist Yugoslavia. And he told us it was a beautiful country with a rich history. Yeah right. I'd believe it when I saw it.
But from then on, my classmates thought my moving was
cool. I was still sad about leaving my friends, but I began to
be curious about my future home.

We left for Croatia a few days before Halloween. My first
sight of the country was the airport. Not very enticing: the
walls were dingy and gray, and the air was filled with ciga-
rette smoke. I couldn't read a single sign since the words
were written in Croatian, which didn't look remotely like the
French or Spanish I'd studied in school. All around me, people
were chatting with words I didn't understand. And just to add
to my already low first impression of the country, the airport
personnel immediately tried to confiscate our dog! When we
went to get Hallie off the plane, they wouldn't let us have
her. We didn't have the foggiest idea what was wrong, and
since we didn't speak a word of Croatian and they didn't
speak a word of English, we had a definite problem. Finally my
dad called a Croatian friend who miraculously convinced the
people at the airport that Hallie wasn't an illegal immigrant,
and we got to take her with us. But I had already decided I
didn't like the place.

Driving from the airport to our new home in the capital

city of Zagreb, the first thing I saw were rows and rows of tall, dilapidated apartment buildings—gray and brown, covered with soot, laundry hanging out to dry on all the balconies. Stucco was peeling off the cracked walls, and there was graffiti everywhere. Scruffy dogs barked as we cruised by. Soon we entered the hilly neighborhood where we would live. The houses were still made of stucco, but they were much nicer. They were all painted bright colors—magenta, purple, blue, orange, yellow, green ... I even noticed a few with stripes! I'd never seen houses like these before. I still wasn't crazy about Zagreb, but I liked the colorful houses. And the snow-capped mountain, *Schljeme*, that rose gently behind the city. So that's why the guidebooks called Zagreb "beautiful." (And here I thought it was because of the dingy apartment buildings.)

When we came to our house, I was surprised to see that it was orange! Unlike our square, brick house in Maryland, this one was shaped like a rectangle and taller than it was wide. When we were inside, my dad showed my sister and me our rooms. They were on the top floor, which previously had been a full apartment for a family of five. There was an eating area, a kitchen, bathroom, living room, and two sleeping "lofts." The lofts were tiny—just a little bigger than a double bed—but having a whole apartment to ourselves was nice.

One week after we arrived, I walked into the American International School of Zagreb. The school was located in what used to be a hospital during the war. It had been renovated on the inside and was new, bright, and friendly-looking. It was small compared to my school in the States— there were only thirteen other students in my grade. And most of those kids were from other countries—France, Germany, Russia, etc. There were only four other students from the United States, but they had lived out of the country for years. These kids had lived all over the world before landing in Zagreb. A typical response, when I asked someone where they were from, was: "Well . . . I was born in Germany, but I've lived in Indonesia, Ethiopia, Kenya, Germany, and Sierra Leone. My sister was born in Pakistan, my mom's Indonesian, and my dad's Austrian." Right.

Probably because these kids had moved and been "new" so many times themselves, they were very friendly. I was invited to go to the movies that first weekend. The theater was in a Zagreb mall called "Kaptol," so I also got to see what a Croatian mall is like. Sadly, like the airport, it was bland and smoky, and there certainly weren't any of my favorite American stores. But everything looks better when you have friends. And I soon did.

Over the next few months, I discovered that I couldn't judge a country by my first impressions. As I learned more about its history, I came to realize that Croatia can't be blamed for its shabby looks. The country doesn't have nearly as much money as America or other Western European countries, so it can't afford to repair all of the damage it suffered during the war. I was amazed to see places that were cordoned off with red tape to alert people that there were still possibly active land mines in the ground there. Across the street, children played handball, accustomed to the danger. I saw half-bombed buildings that were still standing and houses without windows and with pipes sticking out, but the cars in the driveways told me people still lived there. And that's just what shows on the outside. Many Croatians told me that "the scars of war are still inside them." The kind you can't see just by looking.

I also learned what the term "second-world country" means. America and most of Europe are "first-world" countries. Basically, we're rich and have tons of opportunities. Croatia, however, is sometimes called a "second-world" country. Although the Croatian people have the same goals and dreams for their lives that we in America have, most don't have enough money to achieve them. One teenage friend of mine finished high school and wants to go to college, but she can't afford to. She can't get a job either because there are hardly any jobs available for young people. An older woman I know has a Ph.D. in chemistry but gives horseback riding lessons because she can't find a job as a chemist. And my friends back home complain about how puny their allowances are!

It amazes me now how much we have in America that we often take for granted, like dishwashers, clothes-dryers, microwave ovens, Mexican restaurants, no-smoking areas, stand-up showers, frozen waffles, Starbucks, SUVs, drive-thrus, and the Gap. Most people in Croatia have never even heard of these American staples. I've seen shoeless Gypsy children (called "Roma" here) on the streets playing music and begging for money. And every spring, the "better off" people of Zagreb put their major trash (like old sinks, refrigerators, or broken sofas and toys) out on the sidewalks, and the Gypsies come by and pick it up in broken-down trucks. They use other people's cast-offs to make furniture and even their homes. I wonder what it's like to sleep on someone else's mattress . . . to open someone else's broken car door to get into your house . . . to sit on someone else's broken chair . . . to get food out of someone else's broken fridge. I'll never forget the Gypsy children walking up and down the street, looking for old, busted toys to play with. I've never seen that back home in Maryland.

I've learned about national pride here in my new home. In spite of their difficulties, Croatians feel enormous pride for their newly independent country. When Croatian skier Janica Kostelic won three gold medals at the Winter Olympics in 2002, there was a rally for her in the main square of Zagreb. Over 250,000 people—a quarter of the nation's population—showed up to celebrate her victory! Billboards everywhere congratulated her. Croatian girls wore their hair in braids like Janica's. Even the schools were let out!

The more I learn about Croatia, the more my first impressions disappear. Like any place, the country has its problems, but I notice them less now. Now I know so many beautiful places, like 600-year-old houses and churches. In a place like Dubrovnik, you can walk along the ancient stone walls of the fortress that guarded the town from raids hundreds of years ago—and again just ten years ago, when soldiers of neighboring Serbia shot down on the town from the surrounding mountains. And the coast is gorgeous! Picture palm trees and turquoise water, and you know only half of how pretty it really is.

But just as important, I've also noticed new things about myself and my family. I'm much better at adapting to new situations than I thought I'd be. I still don't speak Croatian, but I've learned you can communicate pretty well with anyone if you smile. Being with kids from all over the world in my school has shown me that our differences are skin-deep— underneath, we all want to make friends, have fun, and be ourselves. I still get annoyed with my siblings sometimes, but since I spend a lot more time with my family here, I've even realized that they can be fun, too.

Living here has shown me that you can't judge other countries, cultures, or people based on first impressions. I just had to look past the walls of the airport. And while I definitely miss Maryland, my old school, and my friends (not to mention central air conditioning, non-smoking restaurants, and good ole American shopping), I'm glad I'll never take those things for granted again. When I return to the U.S., I know that I'll see it through different eyes. But that's a good thing (I think). Will the U.S. look foreign or familiar to me? How *will* I see it when I return? I'm not sure. But I do know that I'll miss my friends and school here. And, believe it or not, I'll miss Croatia.

Chapter 6

Terror in My Father's Homeland and in Mine

From: Andrew Chibani
Age: 13 years old
Where: Lebanon

In 1999 my family and I took a trip to my dad's native country, Lebanon. That trip made a profound and lasting impression on me. With its ancient sites and recent history, and its cultural and geographic diversity, Lebanon is a unique and fascinating country.

Some of the oldest cities in the world are in Lebanon; for instance, the ancient city of Byblos, from which the Phoenicians first set sail into the Mediterranean to trade with far-away lands. They traded a rare purple dye made from snail shells gathered off the beaches of Sidon and Tyre; the purple dye became the color of royalty. And the giant cedars of Lebanon were harvested and traded to be made into boats.

Many civilizations have passed through Lebanon since the Phoenicians founded their first cities in 3000 B.C., leaving behind traces of their cultures. The Greeks and Romans left their temples and gods; the Turks gave Lebanon mosaics and fountains. But recent times haven't been kind to Lebanon. On our 1999 visit, I learned not only about the history of Lebanon but also about the future of my own country.

The first thing I noticed about Lebanon was the guns. When we landed in the Beirut International Airport, I saw heavy security everywhere. Soldiers carried M-16 and AK-47 machine guns.

"Dad, why do they all have guns?" I asked.

"Because of the war," he said.

Oh, yeah. Dad had told me many times about Lebanon's 15-year civil war. It had ended in 1990, when I was just one year old.

"And because of terrorism," he finished.

Terrorism? Now that was a concept I didn't totally understand back then. I lived in America, after all, and there hadn't

been a war or any kind of attacks during my lifetime. You didn't see much security or many guns in America back in 1999, but in our travels around Lebanon, the guns were something I quickly got used to.

You can see signs of Lebanon's long history even today because of the country's great diversity. As we walked out of the airport to meet my father's family, we saw women and men dressed in every variety of Middle Eastern traditional clothing, as well as the latest fashions from Paris and New York. Just ahead I could see the happy faces of at least thirty of my Lebanese relatives waiting to welcome us home. I received hundreds of hugs and kisses mixed with tears of joy. Then we formed a caravan of cars and headed up to the mountains to my father's village.

Driving through Beirut, I could see collapsed buildings and roads with big holes in them, and we were stopped at security checkpoints by soldiers who looked at our identification and the contents of the car. We sped along steep, narrow roads though little villages, where we saw many tanks and military trucks.

"What happened, Dad?" I asked.

"It's all from the civil war. This whole country has been a battlefield and much of it has been destroyed. The government still hasn't rebuilt it all."

As we drove past piles of rubble and open buildings, my dad told me about his childhood. When he was my age, his family would go on beach vacations. He loved swimming in the Mediterranean with his brothers, until it became too dangerous when the civil war broke out in 1975. Everyone stayed home to be safe because they were too afraid to travel. Sometimes it would be safer to leave your home and go live somewhere else. When he was eighteen, my father left his home and family in Mreijat for a new life and home in the United States of America. When he was done with his stories, my dad looked out at Beirut sadly. "It's all different now."

We finally reached my grandparents' home in the village of Mreijat. There, overlooking the Bekaa Valley, stood a hundred-year-old stone building, built into the side of a mountain, with a tiered orchard for a front yard. What a beautiful view! From where I stood, the countryside looked so peaceful—no signs of war. When we entered the house the *haflee*

(party) began. Family and friends gathered to celebrate our safe return home with a feast, music, and dance.

During our visit to Lebanon,

we traveled to many historic and beautiful
sites. We drove high up into the mountains
past Beirut to visit the birthplace of the
famous writer and painter Kahlil Gibran.
Gibran was passionate about his love of coun-
try and family. His writings taught love and peace. It's amazing how a country that produced a writer like Gibran could
also be torn with terror and war.

"Dad, it's too bad Lebanese people didn't learn from
Kahlil Gibran's writing," I said. "If they loved Lebanon as
much as he did, there never would have been a war."

"You're right, Andrew. Everyone could have lived happily
together in this beautiful land," my dad said. "During most of
my life, the Lebanese people have been recovering from the
war, but the scars are still visible, right alongside some of the
most beautiful places I have ever seen."

We went to visit my dad's high school, the Jesuit
Academy. It was a giant stone building perched atop a hill,
overlooking the city of Zahle. Dad said, "Andrew, I remember
playing basketball in the schoolyard and the priest chasing us
back into the classrooms." Suddenly, a white-haired priest
came out of the building calling my dad's name. My father
recognized him and they hugged and laughed. My dad was
amazed that they remembered each other after all those
years!

The priest asked, "How would you like a tour of your
father's school?"

"That would be great!" I replied. We toured the old building that is still a boys' school today as the priest told us stories of my dad's school days. He described how sometimes
the school was closed because the city was being bombed

and it wasn't safe for the students to leave home. I couldn't imagine anything like that happening in the United States.

When I returned home from Lebanon, I still didn't understand entirely what the word "terror" meant. I had heard my father's stories and the fears of his Lebanese relatives, but I still had no idea how they felt. Then came September 11th. The terrorist attacks on New York City cleared up my confusion. Suddenly, I could see what has been going on in Lebanon for years and what the people there have survived. Now I understand how terror can practically destroy a country.

People in Lebanon have been living with terrorism all their lives, while in America we just found out what terror was after September 11th, 2001. While normal life in America was disrupted for a while, most Americans still go on with everyday life—shopping at the mall, going to school, even flying on airplanes again. In Lebanon, every time a plane lands safely, the people on board cheer as if they have just won a football game. They are happy they can finally return to a peaceful homeland.

I used to think that America could never be attacked like Lebanon. Now I know better. It can happen at any time to any country. When I saw on the news the bombed-out hole at Ground Zero, I couldn't help remembering the destruction of downtown Beirut. Maybe someday I'll tell my children about the World Trade Center and what America was like before terrorism. September 11th and my visit to Lebanon reminded me how much I love and appreciate my country, the U.S.A. I will never take it for granted.

God bless the United States of America.

Chapter 7

Mi Vida en Sueños (My Life in Dreams)

From: Hannah Jackson
Age: 15 years old
Where: Ecuador

I won't say my travel adventure was one-of-a-kind, but I am confident in saying it wasn't your average vacation. Last summer, my best friend Rachel and I were invited by a friend of my family's to spend a month in Ecuador. We would help on her eco-farm, and in exchange we would get to see Ecuador in a different way than most tourists. I don't think I knew what I was getting myself into. I thought it would be a fun trip, but I never expected it to have such a severe impact on my views on life.

Our parents gave us the go-ahead, and we were thrilled to accept. I mean, an opportunity like that doesn't come around every day! After much shopping and other preparations—buying our plane tickets, getting our vaccinations, buying supplies—it was finally time to go.

Rachel and I flew by ourselves, and Sharon (the family friend) met us at the airport in Quito, the capitol of Ecuador. The eco-farm was a three-hour bus ride from Quito, through various environments: desert, farmland, and rainforest. The eco-farm was called *Sueños*, which means "dreams" in Spanish. Sueños, like all eco-farms, uses methods that are friendly to the environment. They don't use pesticides or other harmful chemicals so as not to do any lasting damage to the earth. At the time of our visit, the farm was still so new that it only produced enough food to feed the people living there, but they hoped to grow enough to sell the surplus within a few years. Many kinds of plants grew there: plantain, cacao, and papaya trees, to name just a few. They were also trying to grow different kinds of vegetables, like carrots, lettuce, and tomatoes. Besides the plant life, there were chickens that laid eggs, plus a whole brood of chicks. They were so cute! We named each one, and eventually we could even recognize which was which!

The farm was pretty rustic. There was cold running water, but not hot, and no electricity. That meant no TV, no stereo, no refrigerator, no microwave, and no telephone. At night we had to read by the dim glow of our flashlights.

We weren't the only people on the farm. During the month we were there, we shared space with seven other guests from the United States who came to stay and work for various lengths of time; several Ecuadorans worked there as well. And there was a resident dog named Melka and a cat who had a new litter of kittens. Life is harsh for animals in Ecuador, especially house pets. Only two out of the five kittens were still alive when we left.

Our closest friend at the eco-farm was Gildardo (pronounced Hill-dárr-doh), who also lived and worked there. He was in his mid-twenties and from Colombia, which he had fled a few years before because of the unrest in that country. After a while, the age and language gap between us didn't matter anymore, and we spent many evenings teaching Gildardo English in exchange for Spanish lessons.

Life on the farm was completely different from anything I had ever experienced. We woke up around 7 A.M.—earlier than I prefer. For breakfast at home we often had oatmeal, granola, or French toast. But in Ecuador breakfast was different. For instance, in our oatmeal, we had plantains (a tropical fruit that is similar to a banana, but better). After breakfast, we headed out to work on the chores.

There is *always* something to be done on a farm: seeds to plant, seedlings to care for, chickens to feed, fruit to pick, coffee to shell. And since Sharon's eco-farm was just getting started, there was also carpentry work to be done. We built a new pen for the chickens and a roof for the laundry area. (I'm sure my friends back home weren't building chicken coops on their vacations.) It was actually a lot of fun. Sadly, my hammering skills did not improve much. Oh well, practice, practice, practice!

Lunch was at noon and almost always included rice. In Ecuador, you eat a *lot* of rice. Other than rice, we'd have

lentils, refried beans, or vegetable soup. And we always had salad as well. After lunch is siesta time! In Latin American countries many people sleep during the hottest part of the day, from noon to two o'clock. In some parts of the world, even the stores are closed while people snooze. (Why don't we do that in the United States?) Rachel and I often spent this time writing letters and postcards, catching up in our journals, reading books, or simply lounging in hammocks. We also went swimming in the river that was practically in our front yard.

One time when we were swimming we saw a *huge* spider on the rocks by the river. It was easily bigger than my out-streched hand. We got out of the water so quickly! Rachel is terrified of spiders, and she wouldn't go back to that part of the water for weeks.

In the afternoon there were more chores, then another communal meal. Everyone took turns cooking the meals, but dinner was the most fun because we had more options of what to make. Rachel and I invented our own dish: pasta with broccoli and spices. Okay, that may sound really boring, but it was delicious. We usually dropped exhausted into bed around eight or nine o'clock, just to wake up the next day at the crack of dawn and start all over again. It was tiring, but we were part of a team. Everyone on the farm helped with the chores, the meals, and the housecleaning. There is so much to be done just to keep a farm going! American kids (including me, before I went to Ecuador) have no idea how easy they've got it.

A couple of times a week, Rachel and I would bike the few miles into Puerto Quito, the nearest town, to run errands. We bought snacks, called home, or just sat and watched the locals go about their business. It was truly fascinating to see how ordinary Ecuadorans lived. Their lives are so different from ours. For one thing, everything in Ecuador was way cheaper than in the United States. A can of soda cost just fifteen cents. You could buy a loaf of bread for six cents. And a three-hour bus ride cost only three dollars! But, the people in Ecuador earn much less money than Americans do. The average American earns about $40,000 a year, while the average Ecuadoran earns just $1,000.

They also expect more of their children in Ecuador. We visited the school on the outskirts of Puerto Quito and helped the students do a little painting. It was a tiny school, with just twenty-five students all together, but the teachers were very good and the children enjoyed school. Many evenings we were visited by Marcos, a child who lived near the farm. Marcos went to school in the morning, worked on his dad's farm in the after-

Continental Airlines
ETKT
NAME: JACKSON/HANNAH
DATE: 23AUG
ONEPASS:
MILEAGE:

FLIGHT: CO 1866Y

GATE: SEAT: 29E
DEPART: 700A ****
QUITO
ARRIVE: 415P ****
NEWARK INTL
BOARD TIME: 615A

noon, and did his homework in the evening. And he was only ten!

Working on the farm was also a great way to get a feel for how Ecuadorans live. One of the most difficult chores I did that month was clearing a field for planting using just a machete. It was hard work! Louis, on the other hand, made it look easy. It was amazing to watch him work. It took all morning for six of us to clear less than half the field. After lunch, Louis cleared the rest of the field by himself . . . in about an hour! He wasn't a very big guy, but man, was he strong.

Watching Louis taught me that if you do something every day, it gets easier. Life on the eco-farm was like that for me. I got used to getting up early, bathing in cold water, reading by flashlight, and doing lots and lots of work. By the end of a month, this totally foreign life felt normal to me. My time in Ecuador also taught me not to take things for granted.

There are so many things I used to count on—electricity, supermarkets, even long daylight hours (in the middle of the summer in Ecuador it was pitch black by 7:30 P.M.!)—that people don't have in many parts of the world. Now that I'm back in the U.S., I've grown accustomed to having these things in my life again, but I don't think I will ever take them for granted like I did before. I would say that my trip to Ecuador was truly one of the most rewarding things I've done in my life. I hope that someday I will be able to return there for another visit—it is such a beautiful and marvelous place. A month there changed everything for me! I'll never look at life the same way again.

Catalina de Erauso

1592 – 1650 + From Spain to Central and South America

You gotta give it to Catalina . . . she had some nerve!
What else can you say about a fifteen-year-old nun who
escaped her convent, dressed up like a man, and pro-
ceeded to travel the world, gambling, fighting, and plun-
dering and pillaging everything in her path? Cool.

Catalina certainly didn't start out as a troublemaker.
She was born to a noble family in northern Spain, and,
like many girls of her class, was sent to live in a convent
at the age of four. No one asked Catalina what she
wanted to do with her life, but back in those days girls
had two choices: become a nun and spend your days in
a convent or become a wife and spend your days at
home taking care of children and chores. Girls were
not allowed to travel or have adventures. That was for
guys only.

Catalina, however, had other ideas. By age fifteen,
she'd had enough of convent life. She wanted out. But
how? Although she knew that a girl on her own would-
n't get far, Catalina ran away. She had a plan. Once she
reached the woods, she chopped off her hair and "with
the blue woolen bodice I had I made a pair of breeches
[pants], and with the green petticoat I wore underneath, a doublet and hose [shirt and socks]—my nun's
habit was useless and I threw it away." *Voilà*—she
was now a *he*.

Dressed as a man, Catalina went off to see the world. At eighteen, she became a soldier in the Spanish army and traveled all over Europe. Next she was off to the Americas, where she and her fellow *conquistadores* invaded Peru and Chile, killing most of the native people and stealing their treasures, all in the name of Spain. How's that for a nice little nun?

For twenty years, Catalina got away with her charade. She knew she had to be constantly vigilant or she'd be discovered. She was sure the King of Spain would either have her killed for her deception, or, worse, make her go back to life as a woman! It wasn't enough to just look like a man; she had to act like one, too, so Catalina took up men's habits of the day—drinking, smoking, playing cards, and fighting. During one card game, a man hurled insults at her, so she stabbed him! To prove her macho nature, the ex-nun killed more than a dozen men with her sword and pistol. She even killed her own brother by accident!

In one particularly nasty duel, Catalina suffered a serious wound. Afraid she was going to die, she confessed her disguise to a Catholic bishop, hoping she'd be forgiven and allowed into heaven. Instead of dying, however, or even going to prison, Catalina was granted a special dispensation from the Pope himself. For her bravery and service to Spain, the Pope forgave her for lying and cross-dressing—*and* allowed her to continue wearing men's clothing! As if that weren't enough, when Catalina returned to Europe in 1624, she was a full-blown celebrity! The King of Spain gave her a generous allowance to live on, and she spent a few years writing a book about her life. Everyone wanted to hear her amazing tale.

Although Catalina was finally living the good life, she couldn't give up her adventurous lifestyle. She headed back to the New World, where she stayed until the end of her days, working as a mule driver in Mexico. From nun, to soldier, to celebrity author, to mule driver. Catalina certainly lived *la vida loca*!

Chapter 8

My Trail of Tears

From: Byron Sun
Age: 16 years old
Where: Guatemala
& the U.S.A.

Los Angeles, California, 1995 ✦ "La Carta"

Mother yelled, "Wake up, my children!"

I opened one eye and looked at the clock; 4 A.M.

"Why do we have to get up so early?" I asked sleepily.

"We're going to the embassy," she said, unraveling her long, black hair from her curlers.

I had been to the U.S. Embassy before. It was always filled with busy, angry people trying to get their paperwork approved. Last month my father received a letter from immi-

69

gration that said my mother and I were approved for visas. That meant we could finally be legal residents here in the United States. Now it was my family's turn to go to the embassy and get *our* paperwork approved.

Driving through the streets of Los Angeles, my parents were laughing and smiling. After seven frustrating years—years of waiting in lines at the embassy, paying a lot of money for documents and lawyers, and living in fear that we would never be a part of our new country—our American dream was finally coming true. My mother and I were going to become U.S. citizens, just like my father and brother. The sunny streets of L.A. looked as hopeful as I felt inside.

As we pulled up to the embassy, however, my stomach sank. The building looked like it was full of bees harvesting their pollen. When I saw the mob of people waiting to get inside, my hands shook. But my mother was laughing like a little kid.

"Let's go in," she said, pulling me by the hand. "We don't have anything to worry about. The letter says that we are approved for visas."

My emotions exploded into a smile, but my dad kept reading the letter over and over, as if he hoped that the words wouldn't change.

Inside the giant building, we made our way through many doors and hallways until we found the correct waiting room. There, we had to take a number and wait our turn. Dad pulled a number: 11. "That is not my lucky number," he said, shaking his head.

Finally a man called, "Number eleven, come in." Mom smiled at me, but her tired eyes betrayed the suffering she had been through to get here. We walked into the office and the man asked to see our paperwork. Very carefully, my dad handed him our precious letter, as if it might break, but the man hardly looked at it. He set it aside and began flipping through a folder. My parents weren't smiling anymore.

"It looks like you've had some trouble with the law."

San Diego, California, 1988 ✦ "Los Mojados"

I don't remember when I first came to California from Guatemala. I was only two years old. All I know is what my mother told me. My father went first, traveling through Mexico and across the U.S. border to my grandfather's house near Los Angeles, California. After a year and a half, Dad saved enough money to pay a "coyote" to bring my mother and me across.

Coyotes are the people who bring illegal immigrants into the United States. Our coyote brought us into the States through an underground sewage tunnel.

My mother told me how she ran with a group of strangers, carrying me tight against her body as she sloshed through rats and excrement. The tunnel was low and dark, so my mother hit her head and dropped me into the mess many times. Her companions helped lift me up and encouraged her to keep going, until finally we reached the end of the tunnel: San Ysidro, California.

Once on American soil, we had to be very quiet and watch out for the immigration patrol. From our hiding place in the bushes, my mother could see dust circling up ahead. A dreadful, green immigration car was coming our way. The coyote grabbed my tiny arm and shook me. "Stay quiet," he hissed.

Maybe I sensed everyone's fear or maybe I was just hungry, but the coyote's warning didn't work: I started to cry. My mother tried muffling my sobs with her hand, but it was no use. They heard me.

All of us—my mother, the kind strangers, and me—were discovered.

The officiers put us in the back of a covered truck and took us to immigration headquarters, where they told Mom to call my father. They said that if he came and paid a thousand dollars, we could go free. My mother knew that if she did what they said my father would be captured, too, so she made no phone call and we spent the night in jail. The next day my father met us in court with a lawyer. He paid the thousand dollars and we got out on bail: temporary freedom.

Before we left, immigration ordered us to return to court in two weeks for a trial. We never went back.

My parents knew that a trial and paperwork would cost a lot more money, but my father had already spent everything he had on the coyote and bail. If we didn't give them more money, they would make us return to Guatemala. My parents decided to take their chances living illegally in America instead.

We made it for seven years.

Los Angeles, California, 1995 ✛ "Malas Noticias"

"Yes," my father finally answered the man. "That was seven years ago when my wife and son first came to

California. Immigration found them in the desert and took them to jail. I paid money so they could get out."

"And you were supposed to go back to court," said the man, "but you didn't." He sounded angry now. "For that, you have to return to your country. You can go voluntarily or we will remove you by force."

Those words ripped into me. Back to Guatemala? How could this be possible? I felt like my world was tearing apart. My brother and I started crying, but my dad sat there speechless and my mom just stared at the letter on the desk, her illusion of a better life vanishing like a mirage.

"You have fifteen days to leave the country," the man said, "or we will come and get you."

Somewhere over Mexico, 1995 ✦ "Despegando de la Tierra"

It was a long flight back to Guatemala. My brother was actually excited because he'd never been on a plane before. But I wasn't excited. I was angry and scared. As we took off from the land that had been our home for seven years, I felt like part of my body was dying.

My parents thought it would be best to go back voluntarily, but since my father was legal in America, he was staying behind. It would be better for him to remain in the U.S. to earn money to support us and to find a way for us to return. I couldn't believe we were going back to Guatemala without him.

That morning Dad had gotten my brother and me out of bed at five. He held us tightly and said, "*Patojos, despiertense. It is time to go.*" It was the first time I had ever seen him cry.

When we left our L.A. apartment, it was completely empty. We had to sell *everything*, even our car and our furni-

UNITED STATES OF AMERICA
DEPARTMENT OF JUSTICE

IMMIGRATION AND NATURALIZATION SERVICE
300 NORTH LOS ANGELES STREET
LOS ANGELES, CA 90012

WARRANT OF DEPORTATION

ture—just to buy the plane tickets and to have a bit of money once we got to Guatemala. After living in the U.S. for seven years, I felt like I was being kicked out of my home. I didn't even remember Guatemala. All the people that I knew and loved, my friends and family, lived in California. I knew California. I knew Disneyland, Universal Studios, and Palm Beach. I did not know Guatemala.

Looking down at the foreign land below me, my mind was filled with questions that couldn't be answered. How would we survive once our money ran out? Where would we live? Would we ever see Dad again?

My mother looked at me and seemed to read my mind. She hugged me and we both cried. She told me not to worry, that Guatemala would be just one more difficult time we would overcome. But I couldn't help feeling that we were moving backwards. After all the struggles and suffering we had gone through to get to America and create a better life for our family, now it was all disappearing behind us. We were going back.

Back to a country my mother hadn't seen for seven years. A country I didn't even remember. Back to a country where we had no home and no money. Back to a country full of crime. Full of drugs. Full of hunger and death. Back to a country in the midst of a civil war. A country where we could easily be killed. Or disappear. We were going back to country where there was no future for our family.

A trail of tears marked our path all the way to Guatemala.

Forest Grove, Oregon, 2003 ✦ "Sabiduria de la Vida"

I spent four long years in Guatemala learning about a way of life that many Americans could not imagine. I saw robberies and murder and poverty. I saw drugs and how they destroy people's lives. I saw people who were so hopeless they no longer had any dreams left inside them.

But I never gave up on my dream of going home, back to America. After four years of being separated from my father, one day we got another unexpected letter in the mail. Dad had gotten our paperwork approved. We were "legal" and flew back to America at last!

Even though I'm an American now, I still keep the lessons of Guatemala inside me. Once I saw a dead man lying in the alley behind our apartment there. He had been murdered, his life taken away in one moment with two bullet shots to the head. For the *Guatemaltecos* who see this every day, it is a way of life. That's just the way it is. But for me, I know that there is a different way. Seeing that dead man made me realize how precious life is and how fragile it can be. Now I try to live life to the fullest every day.

Ironically, some people who make it out of that life can forget its lessons. When they finally get "the good life," some people become selfish in return. One family friend likes to brag about his possessions and yells if you drop something on the floor. He has forgotten what is truly valuable in life. But I have not forgotten. One day I will take my children to Guatemala so that they can see where our family came from. So they can appreciate what we have but also know what others are missing.

Chapter 9

Boot Camp

From: Pamela Edgeworth
Age: 16 years old
Where: U.S.A

It was the summer between my freshman and sophomore years, and all of us in Junior ROTC at Proviso High School were getting excited about the upcoming "Boot Camp" being hosted by the U.S. Navy. Master Chief (one of the leaders of our ROTC group) could only pick fifteen students to go. At our next meeting, Master Chief told us who the lucky students would be. When I heard him say my name, I could hardly believe it. I was going to Boot Camp! I ran home as fast as I could to tell my parents the good news.

Mom grinned when I told her. "What are you going to

need for the trip?" she asked, giving me a big hug.

Dad was happy for me, too, but also a bit worried. "They're going to be screaming in your face for the whole week," he warned. "Are you going to call home crying, begging to come back?"

I shook my head no.

"You sure you can handle it, Pamela?" he asked. "It's going to be tough."

"I can handle it," I answered. At least I thought I could. But what did I know about Boot Camp? I just knew that I wanted to join the Navy or Air Force when I graduated.

It took me almost a week to get ready, but finally my "big day" arrived. I was so excited, I got to school early, before anyone else. When the other cadets started arriving, we all sat looking around our meeting room nervously, wondering what was going to happen to us over the next seven days.

Master Chief and Commander (our other ROTC leader) walked in looking happy. They knew what was going to happen to us, but they weren't telling.

We walked outside to the bus and said good-bye to our parents. My mother kissed and hugged me until the very minute it was time to go.

"Keep your head up!" she yelled as I got on the bus. "And don't call home crying!"

Then we were off. As we pulled up to the gate of the reserve base, Master Chief told us, "Don't worry, you're going to have a good time," so we relaxed and started laughing and making jokes. Then Master Chief got off the bus and a marine got on. The marine, however, was not pleased by our relaxed attitude. He started cursing and made us do "double time" (running fast) off the bus and into "formation" (standing in columns at attention).

Looking around the base, I could see that there were lots more schools there than just mine. There must have been hundreds of other students getting off buses. It was a crazy scene with everyone grabbing their luggage and running to where they were supposed to be. Soldiers were barking out loud orders all around me, hurrying people along. Now I was truly scared. Already I wanted to call home. But then I remembered what my mom said: Keep your head up. If I couldn't last a week at Boot Camp, how could I make it into the Navy or the Air Force? I wouldn't call home, no matter what.

That first night, dinner surprised me. We all expected the food to be terrible, but the fried chicken and mashed potatoes were actually delicious. The showers were another story. We shared a bathroom with lots of other cadets, so I had to wait in a line just to clean up. All of us slept in big, long, dormitory-style rooms; girl cadets in one wing, boy cadets in another. Every morning we had to make our beds and keep all our stuff in order. I wasn't used to that kind of life, but it was fun getting to know other girls in my barracks.

I was homesick the first day, but by the second day I was too focused on camp to think about anything else. We had to wake up at 0500 hours (five o'clock in the morning) and get ready for PT (physical training), where we did push-ups, ladder kicks, jumping jacks, and even ran a mile and a half. What a way to wake up! Then we had to do double time back to the barracks, put on our uniforms (khaki pants, shirt, and hat, plus black patent-leather shoes), then do double time back outside for the flag salute and Pledge of Allegiance. Only after all that did we finally get to eat breakfast!

We spent the rest of the day doing all kinds of fun stuff. Orienteering was my favorite. Our platoon would march into the woods, where they taught us how to use a compass and read maps, and then we had to find our way back out. We also swam and drilled against other platoons, testing how well we could march and do formation and whether we knew all the commands. We even learned how to shoot an M-16! I was surprised when I was the first one in my platoon to hit the target. For the whole week, we had to live without TV, music, or telephones. It wasn't easy. I was used to that stuff and missed it. But I was so busy meeting new people and learning new things every day that I had no time to worry about it.

By the last day of camp we were ready for graduation. I could see my mother and my friends' parents from the stands. My dad couldn't make it, but I knew he was there in spirit. At the end of the ceremony, Master Chief and Commander walked up to us, the ROTC students of Proviso, and congratulated us on our accomplishment: "We are very proud of you. You achieved a lot, and you are now an official unit." We had made it!

Our parents were proud of us, too, and happy to see that we had survived. They were amazed at how dark our skin had gotten from being out in the sun every day. After graduation, we ran and jumped into their arms, hugging and kissing them just like on that first day when we left for Boot Camp. As we loaded onto the bus to go home, I was sad to leave because I had had such a good time and was just getting to know the other cadets. I couldn't believe it, but I almost cried because I missed Boot Camp already. On the bus ride back, everyone was real quiet; not like the laughing and joking on the way there. I guess I wasn't the only one who was sad to leave.

Although we were sad, we were also relieved to be going home to our beds and TVs and the noise of the street. Walking into my house, I smiled at my dad.

"So how was Boot Camp? Did you have fun?" he asked.

I told him all about PT, the drills, the orienteering, and everything else I had done.

"You really did have fun," he said, amazed.

I remembered what he'd said to me when I was leaving for camp. He was right: they did scream in our faces the whole week. And I did want to call home and beg to come back. But I stayed strong. I kept my head up and made it to the end. Boot Camp was a challenge I never could have gotten anywhere else. Not only was it a fun experience but it helped me focus on my goals and build my self-confidence. I guess I do have what it takes to go for my dreams.

For the rest of that summer, I was glad be home. I was so worn out that I must have slept about four extra hours every day. And I kept shining my Boot Camp shoes so they wouldn't wear out—I might need them in the future.

Chapter 10

The Great Escape

From: Alison Safran
Age: 10 years old
Where: U.S.A.

Dear Diary,

Finally, my first day of camp! I've been looking forward to going
to Camp Eisner for months. It's a camp for Jewish kids like me,
but it's not just about religion. We get to do all kinds of stuff.
That's why I came. I can't believe I almost *didn't* come. I'm only
eight years old, so I wasn't sure if I could handle being away
from home at a sleep-away camp for a whole month. But in the
end I decided that I am totally mature enough to handle being
on my own. Plus, my friend Zoe is here, too, so I'm not com-

pletely alone. And there's a ton of fun activities here: listening to the radio, making art, and, of course, swimming and kayaking, two of my favorite things.

In fact, I was so busy today, I didn't get sad at all. Even saying good-bye to my mom when she dropped me off didn't make me cry (though I'm sure it would have if she'd stayed a minute longer). Although this is my first time away from home and from my family for more than a few days, I'm completely excited. And maybe just a little scared, too.

Your happy camper,
Alison Safran

Dear Diary,

It's after midnight and I'm still awake. Why, you ask? Because there are three girls in my cabin who snore! That's why. Plus, at home I have my own room and my own very soft bed. I hate the lumpy, 2-inch mattresses here and I'm not used to sleeping with other people all around me. Especially when those people sound like they're mowing the lawn so loudly that I can't even hear myself think. This is the worst. Not to mention that I have to get up in just a few hours! Ugh.

Sleepily yours,
Alison

Dear Diary,

Today I officially got homesick. I miss the food and the people back home. When I first got sad a few tears leaked out. I pretended it was nothing and told people I had sunblock in my eyes. But at Torah study, about halfway through the game we were playing, I gave up. I couldn't take it anymore. I mean, how long did I really think people would believe the sunblock excuse? Who would have sunblock in their eyes for a whole month? I started really bawling.

At first, I don't think anyone saw me; I tried to hide behind my counselor Bobbi (her real name is Robin, but she likes to be called Bobbi). Then Bobbi turned around and asked me what was wrong. I can't remember what I said—in fact, I probably didn't say anything because I was still crying.

She took me over to the water fountain by the nurse's office (which we call "the infirmary" for some reason), and I told her what was wrong. I said the only words I could bear to say without crying even harder: "I miss my family." Bobbi gave me a hug and said, "You'll be fine."

Later Zoe saw me crying and asked, "What's the matter, Ali?"

"I'm homesick," I answered.

Zoe also said, "You'll be fine."

I'm not so sure about that.

Just a teensy bit homesick,
Alison

Dear Diary,

It's only the third day of camp and I'm crying again. It's not
that camp is so horrible. I mean we do get to have Shabbat
and swim, but I feel like something's missing... like I should-
n't have come to camp. I miss my brother and sister the
most... even more than my parents. I really just want to go
home. Now.

This morning a counselor took me into the kitchen,
plonked me down on the metal counter *really hard*, and
barked, "You have to stop crying." I barked back, "I can't!" I
seriously wanted to put *her* on the counter and tell *her* to
leave me alone! Then my unit leader gave me her stuffed frog
for comfort. The frog, I'm sorry to say, didn't help. Nothing is
helping, actually, and I'm miserable. It's time for desperate
measures. It's time to think up a way to escape this place.
Hmmm ... maybe I could get a map at free time. You know,
so I don't get lost if I walk home. Or I could take a counselor's car ... but I can't drive, and heck, I'm only four feet
tall! There is no way I could reach the pedals.

Ah ha! I've got it. Just wait until tomorrow ...

Your scheming, homesick friend,
Alison

Dear Diary,

I'm sorry to say it, but Escape Plan #1 did not go so well.
Today I pretended to have laryngitis. I was sure that being
sick would get me home 21 days earlier than the rest of the

group—but appar-ently not. When I woke up this morning, I whispered to my counselor, "I can't talk." She went along with it . . . maybe she even believed me at first. All through breakfast, I kept quiet, using sign language to get food passed to me.

After breakfast, I went to the infirmary where the nurse gave me one of those popsicle-stick tests. When she asked my name, my cabin mate Emma (who was in on the plan), answered for me: "Her name is Alison." The nurse asked why I didn't answer for myself. "She has laryngitis," Emma said quickly, making a good recovery. "She can't talk." The nurse seemed to believe us. So far my plan was working like a charm. I figured I'd be home in no time.

But right before dinner, I started laughing when one of my friends told a joke. My counselor heard me and said, "People with laryngitis *cannot* laugh." She smiled a very sly smile. "In fact, people with laryngitis can't talk *at all*! Not even a whisper." I'd been whispering all day . . . maybe even louder than a whisper! I thought I'd put on a good perform- ance, but I guess not. Oops!

At dinner the other counselors kept giving me disap- pointed looks, like they couldn't believe I'd try to escape camp in such a lame way.

Now everyone knows I faked the laryngitis. My plan totally failed. Guess I'll just have to come up with something else.

Yours in silence,
Alison

Dear Diary,

Guess what? Zoe and I came up with *the* best escape plan!
Today during stories and coloring period, we took paper and
markers and wrote letters home. Mine said:

> *Dear Mom and Dad,*
> *I need to come home. I'm scared, sad, and I wake up at 5 A.M.*
> *every morning because I can't sleep here. I miss you, and I'm*
> *not ready for sleep-away camp. Please come pick me up this*
> *Saturday at 1:15 in the afternoon. You don't need to talk to*
> *the camp before you do this, just please please please please*
> *please come pick me up. Remember, THIS SATURDAY AT*
> *1:15 P.M. PLEASE COME PICK ME UP!!!!!!*
>
> *Love,*
> *scared, sad, needs-to-be-picked-up, Ali*

We put our notes into envelopes and our fates were
sealed, literally (as in sealing the envelopes). I'm so relieved.
My parents could never leave me here after reading that. I'll
be home in a few days!

Homeward bound,
Alison

Dear Diary,

What can I say? It's Saturday, it's nine at night, and I'M STILL AT CAMP!!! It seems that Escape Plan #2 has failed as well. Not that Zoe and I did anything wrong. At lunchtime we sat smiling at each other at our table. We couldn't wait for 1:15! We chose Saturday (today) at 1:15 for the pickup because this is the day we have four hours of free time. Four whole hours when our counselors would not be around to see us leave! I was so proud of us and our brilliant plan. I was sure we couldn't fail.

After lunch it was singing time. Uh-oh. I had completely forgotten about singing time! I worried that we wouldn't make it back to the cabin in time for our parents. Would our families leave if we weren't there? I looked down at my watch. 1:09. Good, I thought, we still have time. Singing time finished at 1:12, and you'd better believe it—Zoe and I raced out of the dining hall as fast as we could go! We ran past the campers, past the counselors, up the steep hill, and back to our cabin. We were panting on our front porch at 1:14. We had a whole twenty seconds to spare!

We sat on the porch and waited. 1:15 came and they didn't show up. Still we waited. 2:15, no show. Still we waited. At 3:15, one of our cabin mates returned with popsicles from the dining hall. I asked if she would bring us some, but she said no. So I made a mad dash to the dining hall, while Zoe watched for our rescuers. Minutes later I returned with two cherry-blueberry-lemon-striped popsicles. But still no parents.

At 4:15 we lost all hope. Why didn't they come? Don't they know the pain I'm feeling? Don't they care? Free time ended at 5:15 and everyone got ready for dinner. I skipped dinner and sat here crying on my bunk instead. I am not a happy girl.

Trapped in the wilderness,
Alison

Dear Diary,

Today's the Fourth of July. It's also my birthday. Not many kids have to spend their birthday at camp, but I did. Since my parents abandoned me here, I was forced to celebrate my ninth birthday without them, so many miles away from my own cozy, 5-inch-mattress bed. Actually, today wasn't *that* bad. When I woke up this morning, I discovered that my counselors had decorated my bed with a sign hanging over me that read: "HAPPY BIRTHDAY ALISON!" They also taped green, yellow, blue, red, and orange balloons to the side of my bunk.

All day long people treated me extra nice. I got the best seat at our dining table, my unit leader (the one who gave me the stuffed frog) decorated my head with star stickers, and I didn't even have to do cleanup! At dinner the whole camp sang "Happy Birthday" to me.

After dinner I got called to the camp office. Uh-oh, I thought. They must have heard about my escape plans and now I'm in trouble! But I was wrong. Since it was my birthday, they just wanted to let me call my parents! I was so excited.

I talked on the phone for ten minutes—I think it was the

longest call I've ever had! I talked to everyone: my mom, my
dad, my little brother, Michael, and my little sister, Caroline.
I asked my mom, "Why didn't you come and get me on
Saturday? Didn't you get my letter?"

"What letter?" she replied.

It's been four days, but they still haven't gotten the letter
yet! I forgot how slow the mail is.

"Do you still want to come home early?" she asked after I
told her about Escape Plan #2.

I thought about it for a minute. Today wasn't so bad . . .
actually, it was kind of good. And Parent Visiting Day was only
a week away. I thought I could at least make it until then.

"No, that's okay, Mom. I think I'll stay a little longer."

When I got back to my cabin, there was a delicious vanilla
cake covered in chocolate frosting waiting for me. Our entire
cabin sat outside in our pajamas, under millions of stars, and
ate it. Tonight I am actually happy!

Happy Birthday to me,
Ali

Dear Diary,

Today was Parent Visiting Day. When I first saw my family, I
started crying again. But not sad tears this time... happy
tears. Mom, Dad, my brother, my sister, and even my cousin
Debbie showed up to visit me and I gave them a tour of
camp. We visited the candy "station" (yummy!), where
campers who wrote letters to their families got candy for
writing them. I've gotten *a lot* of candy the past few weeks! I

showed them the
outdoor sanctuary,
the soccer field, the
ropes course, the
tower I climbed, and
my cabin.

When Visiting
Day was over, I
walked my family
back to our car and
asked my dad how much time was left until the end of camp.
"Only 172 hours left," he said. I told him that I thought I
could probably make it that long. Probably.

It was so great to see them. They even left me presents—
a book, the latest *American Girl* magazine, and a Ring Pop
candy! There's no stopping my happiness. And you know what
else they left me? Tonight, when I got into my bunk, I found a
note under my pillow. It said:

Dear Alison,

*It's Saturday night and we are all so excited to see you
tomorrow! By the time you get this card, we'll have had our
visiting day and you'll have just a few sweet days of camp left
before you head home. Dad and I are so thrilled to know that
you are loving your experiences at Eisner, and we are so very
proud of you for hanging in there to get through the first very
rough days. I hope that it helps you to know the part of you
that is strong as an ox, brave as a lion, and wise as an owl to
face whatever you need to in life and come out the other side*

strong and happy and full of possibility! Enjoy your Monday,
Tuesday, Wednesday, Thursday, Friday (Shabbat!), Saturday,
and we'll see you Sunday!

With love and hugs and hearts full of joy,
Mom and Dad

A very happy camper,
Ali

Dear Diary,

Sorry I haven't written in you all week, but I've been having
too much fun. I learned how to swim like a fish. I'll try to
write more later, but I only have 63 hours left!

Your friend,
Ali

Dear Diary,

Today was my last day at camp. Wow! The month sure flew by
fast. And I'm proud to say that I'm leaving the same day as
everyone else. As I stood outside our cabin with Zoe, surrounded by campers and their bags, I scanned incoming
license plates looking for our numbers. When I saw it—a
Massachusetts plate with 3 numbers and 3 letters on it—I
almost screamed.

   Our car had signs on all the windows . . . signs for me! "I
LOVE AKS!" said one. "ALISON'S HOME!" said another one,

decorated with a rainbow and a sun. A quick hug for Zoe, then I tossed my duffel bag into the trunk and we drove away. Finally.

As I sit here writing in you on my own comfortable bed, in my own quiet room, I realize that I'm glad I didn't escape from Camp Eisner after all. I'm so glad I went and got to experience the fun, the smiles, and even the sad moments of camp. And I proved myself wrong; I *could* survive a month away from home, away from my family. I am a firecracker, just like my birthday: bright and full of surprises. I'm happy to be back, of course, but I'm actually thinking about going to sleep-away camp again. But not next year. Maybe in a few years, when I'm twelve or thirteen, I'll be mature enough to survive that snoring! Maybe, but I'm not promising anything just yet . . . those girls snored pretty darn loud!

Love,
Ali

Sacagawea

1789 – 1812 ✦ From North Dakota to the
Pacific Ocean

Can you imagine having to hike, paddle, and ride horse-back halfway across the United States, surrounded by nothing but a bunch of smelly guys? Now strap a new-born baby to your back and you'll know how sixteen-year-old Sacagawea must have felt. This was no luxury vacation. But Sacagawea wasn't used to luxury. In fact, she'd had such a tough childhood that she might have thought the journey with Lewis and Clark was fun by comparison.

First she was kidnapped from her tribe, the Shoshones, by a warring tribe from the east, the Hidatsas. They forced the twelve-year-old girl to walk hundreds of miles—from what is now Idaho to North Dakota—to their village. A few years later a French fur trader named Toussaint Charbonneau won Sacagawea in a game of cards! Ever the romantic, Charbonneau took the young teen as his wife and soon they had a child, Jean Baptiste Charbonneau, later nicknamed Pomp.

But Sacagawea was one tough girl. In 1804, when Captains Meriwether Lewis and William Clark swept into town, talking about exploring the land west of the Mississippi for the President of the United States and about their need for guides and interpreters, Sacagawea jumped at her chance. They hired her husband as a guide, but really Lewis and Clark wanted Charbonneau's wife to help translate and make peace with the various Indian tribes they would encounter on the trip. Sacagawea strapped Pomp to her back in a traditional Indian cradleboard, and never looked back. After years of slavery, Sacagawea was heading west, toward her homeland.

It didn't take long for her to realize the limitations of her fellow travelers. The illustrious Corps of Discovery was really just a ragtag bunch of men with little or no knowledge of local plants, animals, geography, or Indian customs. On the long grueling journey through what is now North Dakota, Montana, Idaho, and Oregon, Sacagawea saved their hides plenty of times. She taught the men how to find and cook edible plants so that they wouldn't starve when their food supplies ran out (which happened more than once). From her memory of the forced march with the Hidatsa kidnappers, Sacagawea guided them safely through areas of which they had no maps or prior knowledge. She also translated for Indian tribes when their languages were similar to her own. But most importantly, during a time when most tribes were understandably hostile to white invaders, Sacagawea's presence reassured the Indians that the group was on a peaceful mission.

Not only did she save their hides, but she even saved those famous journals that Lewis and Clark used to record their historic journey. The group was canoeing through a pretty rough patch of river rapids when one of the boats began to capsize. The men panicked as their precious supplies, including the journals, started floating away. Only young Sacagawea stayed calm. The men stared in shock as she dove overboard—with Pomp still strapped to her back—and rescued the journals!

Lewis and Clark were even more grateful to have Sacagawea on their trip when they finally reached Shoshone country. They somehow had to get through the Bitterroot Mountains next, but they couldn't do it without more horses, supplies, and directions. When the Shoshones first saw the white men coming, they considered killing them but changed their minds when they noticed an Indian girl with them. It turned out that in the years Sacagawea had been away, her brother Cameahwait had become chief of the tribe! The Corps of Discovery stayed as guests of the Shoshone for an entire month, and when they left, Chief Cameahwait gave them food, horses, detailed instructions, and a Shoshone guide to lead them through their passage over the mountains. Although Sacagawea was torn, she decided to continue on with Lewis and Clark. She wanted to finish the journey.

They reached the Pacific Ocean and the end of their outward journey in November 1805. With Sacagawea's help, they had explored more of the west than any group of European travelers before them. Sacagawea traveled thousands of miles—across mountains, down rivers, and even over waterfalls—carrying a baby and the hopes of a new nation on her strong back. Without their teenage guide, it is likely that the illustrious Corps of Discovery would have died before discovering anything.

Remember that the next time you pull a shiny gold Sacagawea dollar out of your pocket.

Chapter 11

What Doesn't Kill You Makes You Stronger

From: Jennifer Payne
Age: 16 years old
Where: Boundary Waters

I sat there on a log, dazed and depressed. The only thing I could think about was how much fun my family thought I was having. What had possessed me to come all the way from hot and sunny South Carolina to the frigid Boundary Waters of Minnesota? I thought back to all the paperwork I had filled out to be able to take this trip, and how happy I was when I heard that I'd been chosen to go. What happened to the sense of adventure that had led me to sign up for this week-long primitive camping trip so far away from home? Had the

mosquitoes sucked that out of me, too? I gritted my teeth. I wasn't going to complain; I was going to tough it out, even if it killed me.

"You know, what doesn't kill you only makes you stronger," one of my fellow campers piped up, after watching me swat at mosquitoes for a while. I grinned. For some reason, her comment made me feel a little better.

Eight of us girls spent that night at base camp. When we woke up at dawn, the real adventure began. We shouldered the backpacks we had stuffed the night before and carried our canoes down to the water, where each team loaded up its boat. After a quick snapshot, we were on our way with no clue of what to expect.

There were three positions in each canoe: bow, stern, and princess. The stern sits in back and guides the canoe with her paddling. She is in charge of turning and steering the boat. The bow rides in front and provides the brute strength. The princess sits in the middle and does nothing. To make up for being "dead weight," the princess must entertain the others. That morning I was princessing, but I didn't know the rule yet.

As we paddled out onto that wide blue water, I just

stared at it. All my fears and worries disappeared with the cool breeze that welcomed us to the Boundary Waters. The mosquitoes that had plagued me at base camp were gone. The only thing that bothered me was the fact that I was doing nothing; however, it didn't take long for my crew to inform me of the princess's important role. I didn't know what to do, but I learned quickly. Soon I could sing camp songs with the best of them, and my princess wave could rival a queen's; however, my stories left a lot to be desired.

We paddled all day and then stopped at several campsites before our guides found one that was worthy. That night we were supposed to have burritos for supper. The person cooking, however, added too much water, and dinner turned into bean soup instead. It was still pretty tasty—a nice hot bowl of bean soup with cheese, cabbage leaves, and tortilla for bread. Man, sign me up!

For dessert we made chocolate pudding—a really big pan full. "This is the life," I thought. Most of our crew refused to touch the pudding because it was made with dehydrated milk and was pretty lumpy. "Awesome! More for us," two brave souls and I declared. We ate it right out of the pan. That night I learned that it is possible to eat too much chocolate pudding. We were doing primitive, low-impact camping, and one major rule is "whatever you pack in, you pack out." Leftover chocolate pudding was not something we wanted to pack out. The three of us had to eat that whole gigantic pan full of pudding.

What doesn't kill you only makes you stronger.

And then there was the Tang. We ate something different at every meal, but we could always count on Tang for break-

fast. Since we were traveling by canoe and couldn't carry enough water for a week, we had to drink lake water. To kill the germs in the water, we poured iodine in it, giving it an overbearing flavor. Most of the time we just drank the iodine water plain, but for breakfast and supper we added Tang for flavoring. And, of course, all our water had texture since we always mixed the iodine and water in old one-gallon ice cream buckets. No matter how careful we were, there was always stuff floating in our drinks.

What doesn't kill you only makes you stronger. And bugs give you protein.

That first night of camping was cold. In addition to my pajamas, I wore a wool sweater and a rain jacket. I was still cold. It was supposed to be summer. I tried pulling my legs up closer to me, but the designers of my mummy-style sleeping bag did not believe in legroom. It seemed like just minutes later that our guides were banging on our tents and singing the "morning song." Time to get up already? I want to go home!

Mosquitoes, also known as "Minnesota State Birds," were always waiting for us on land. They descended upon us like a dark blood-sucking cloud. I had welts everywhere—on my face, my toes, my elbows . . . even on my scalp! I couldn't even scratch because I was too sunburned. One of my crewmates got bit on her eyelid, and it swelled up so much that she couldn't see out of that eye for three days. Those mosquitoes had no mercy.

What doesn't kill you only makes you stronger.

When we weren't eating, drinking iodine water, or killing mosquitoes, we were paddling. There were only two things that broke up long hard chunks of paddling: lunch and portages. To eat lunch, we pulled our canoes up to a rock big enough for all of us to sit. Out came the rye crackers, onions, and cheese. Every lunch was the same. But it was rather pleasant to take a break, guzzle iodine water, and chat.

The portages were another matter. A "portage" is a place where there is no water connecting the lakes and rivers. To get from one body of water to another, you have to carry all your packs, canoes, paddles, life jackets, and water bottles over the land. Some portages are short—maybe a two-minute walk—but others are miles long and torturous. Your muscles strain as mosquitoes bite you. But you can't brush them off because you're carrying a canoe over your head.

On the third portage, I decided it was time for me to carry a canoe. Before that, I had always carried a pack, plus other gear. Of course, for my first time carrying a canoe I chose the rockiest portage yet. I wasn't sure I could carry the big metal canoe by myself for such a long distance, but I wanted to try.

To carry a canoe, you flip it upside down and balance

Sticky Moose

There was a sticky moose
Repeat
He liked to drink a lot of juice
Repeat
There was a sticky moose
Repeat
He liked to drink a lot of juice
Repeat

Chorus:
Singin' Oh-Wah-O
Repeat
Wah-O-Wah-O-Wah-O-Wah-O
Repeat
Wah-O-Wah-O
Repeat
Wah-O-Wah-O-Wah-O-Wah-O
Repeat

His drank his juice with care
But he spilt some on his hair
Chorus
He drank his juice in bed
But he spilt some on his head
Chorus
Now he's a sticky moose
A sticky moose all full of juice
Now he's a sticky moose
A sticky moose all full of juice!
Chorus

each edge on your shoul-
ders, with your head in
the middle of the canoe.
This is called "flipping
up." We counted to
three, then I flipped
the canoe up over my
head. It came to rest
on my shoulders,
where it swayed and
seemed very unbalanced. I

shifted it around a bit. It wasn't heavy, and strangely
enough, it felt right.

The portage was not a smooth walk. Rocks jutted out
everywhere. It would be easy to fall, even without an oddly-
balanced canoe on your head. I stared at the ground, carefully picking my way. A group of guys had stepped off the trail
to let us pass. They were sitting on a rock, watching us go by.

"Look at that girl," said one, pointing at me.

"You know it's a five-mile portage, don't you?" sneered
the tallest one, his voice full of superiority.

"Yeah, right," I said under my breath. Did he think I could-
n't read a map?

"Don't fall," said another, laughing. "We wouldn't want
you to hurt yourself."

I brushed past them.

"You okay, Jennifer?" my guide asked.

"Just fine," I huffed. And I truly was. I tuned the guys out
and focused on picking my steps, leaping from rock to rock
with a grace those guys could only wish for—even if they

were just plain walking. We cracked ourselves up singing "I
Am Woman" as loud as we could, and we finished the
portage in record time.

What doesn't kill you only makes you stronger.

Our last day on the water was unforgettable. There was a
powerful headwind—a wind that blows directly against your
course. They say when you have headwinds as you leave the
Boundary Waters, it's because the waters don't want you to
go. Huge waves crashed against our canoe, and I had to dig
into the water with all of my strength. Still, it felt like we
were moving in place. I couldn't stop paddling or we would
lose any distance we had gained.

The canoe slapped down hard against the incoming
waves, throwing us up in the air and drenching me from head
to toe. Sweat soaked my shirt and trickled into my eyes,
making it difficult to see. My arm muscles burned and my
back ached, but our canoe kept moving forward. Finally I
could see base camp on the shore and I realized that the trip
hadn't killed me after all. Not the food. Not the cold. Not
the portages. Not even the mosquitoes. As I paddled those
last few minutes, the wind tugged at my hair, tossing it behind
me, and I grinned up at the sky. I felt beautiful. But more than
that, I felt strong.

Chapter 12

Puppy Road Trip

From: Bobby Frank
Age: 13 years old
Where: Florida

My name is Bobby, and this is the funny story of how I got my dog Bubba.

My family was arguing about whether or not we should get a dog; the discussion had been going on for more than six months. My mom wasn't sure she liked the idea. She would ask questions like "Who is going to take care of this dog?" and "What would we do with the dog when we go out of town?" I promised her that I would take care of the dog. She finally softened up and said she would consider getting a dog only if it was an "outside" dog. She was worried about dog hair and dog smell inside our house. My parents had a golden retriever before I was born and Dad really wanted another one, but Mom felt they were "too big" and had "way too much hair!" I hate to say it, but Mom was outvoted by the rest of the family. We started looking for a golden retriever.

Our search began by talking to different breeders and searching on the Internet. My dad and I found a breeder located in Portland, Oregon, that has a reputation for raising top-of-the-line, champion dogs. Her dogs are known for winning field and trial competitions. Basically, that means her dogs have the best instincts for hunting and retrieving, which was important for Dad and me since we like to hunt birds. We called and ordered a male puppy and gave him the name Bubba (that's the nickname people call Dad and me). Bubba's mom, dad, and grandparents were all field champions. He had just been born, so we had to wait six weeks before he would be old enough to be put into a crate and flown by air cargo from Oregon across the country to Florida.

One week went by . . . then two . . . then three . . . then four . . . then five. Finally the sixth week came and I was so excited. The lady from Oregon called and told us Bubba was ready to leave his mom. It was in the summer, and the airlines won't fly animals when the temperature is over 85 degrees. We live in Florida, so you can imagine how hot it was in July. We tried to get the breeder to fly Bubba to us several times, unsuccessfully. To avoid the heat, animals are usually flown only at night. To fly across the country from Oregon to Florida, Bubba would have had to change flights several times. It couldn't all be done in one night, but he couldn't fly during the day because the temperature would be too hot. We were stuck. Finally my dad came up with a brilliant plan. We got to fly him as far as they could with the temperature rule, which was to Atlanta, Georgia. That was still 500 miles away from us.

Bubba was due to arrive in Atlanta at 6 A.M. the following morning. Next thing I knew, my dad came home around dinnertime and said, "ROAD TRIP! We're going to Atlanta!" I was so happy that our puppy was finally on a plane and I would actually be able to hold him in my arms in less than twenty-four hours. I just couldn't believe it! The excitement of driving so far to pick him up was also cool. I was grinning from ear to ear.

My dad and I packed our bags and headed off to Atlanta within thirty minutes. It was a long seven-hour drive. To pass the time on the drive we listened to music and talked about what Bubba would look like and how he would act when we picked him up at the airport. We wondered if he would be hungry or thirsty and what condition the inside of the crate would be in. We drove into Atlanta at 1:30 A.M. and headed towards the airport. We located a hotel just outside the airport, checked in, and finally got to sleep at 2:30. Next thing I knew, I was blasted awake by an alarm: BEEP BEEP BEEP! My dad told me, "All right, it's 5:30. We'd better get going if we have to pick him up by 6:30." Ugh! I thought. But then we were off! After going around the airport about five times, we finally found the air cargo building.

The building was small. Inside, there was a long chute, like a slide, that all the boxes came down on, into the freight room. Dad and I spotted an animal crate in the middle of all the boxes. It was Bubba! My heart was pounding as we went to pick him up. He was the cutest dog in the whole entire world. He was very small and had a slightly long nose and the funniest kinky hair behind his ears. He looked like a mad scientist.

We put Bubba in the back seat, shut the door, and got in the car. As soon as we closed the doors, I said, "What is that awful smell?" We turned around and saw that Bubba had gone poop all over in his crate. We quickly started the car and put our heads out the windows. The nearest rest stop was forty-five minutes away, so we drove for forty-five minutes with our heads out the windows.

At the rest stop, we pulled up next to a hose, got out of the car, and took Bubba out of his crate. I held him on his leash while my dad cleaned out his crate. Next we gave him a bath, dried him off, and put fresh newspaper in his crate. Finally my dad and I went to the restroom to wash our hands. Problem solved.

But when we got back to the car, Bubba had pooped in his

crate again! We were soaked and exhausted and mad because
we had to clean everything all over again. After we dealt with
clean-up number two, we took Bubba to the restroom with
us. While my dad washed his hands, I stood outside with the
puppy. Then Dad and I switched places.

Once again, we hit the road. We drove and drove, until I
asked, "When will we be home?" and my dad said, "Ten minutes." Finally we pulled up to our house and my mom, dad,
sister, and I finally got to play with our new puppy.

In spite of the smelly accident, it was a great road trip. I
still have my dog Bubba, who is three years old now and very
playful, even though he's not a puppy anymore. I'm glad I got
my dog because when I can't find anything to do, I can play
with him and we have lots of fun. I love Bubba because he
has brought joy to my life—we play fetch and tug-of-war
together, and we also go for walks (occasionally). Bubba
loves to wake me up in the morning with a big lick on my
face. Since that first trip, Bubba has traveled many other
places with us. But he doesn't poop in the car anymore.

Thank goodness!

George Washington Carver
ca. 1865 – 1943 ✦ From Missouri to Alabama

Who in the world would walk hundreds of miles just to
go to school? George Washington Carver, that's who.
When he was twelve years old, George left home and
walked across much of the southern United States in
search of an education. He didn't stop walking and
learning until he was in his thirties and had earned a
master's degree. Not an easy task for a black man in the
south!

It seemed that George was destined for travel from
the very start. George, his brother, and his mother lived
in Missouri and were owned by Moses and Susan
Carver. But when George was just a baby, he and his
mother were kidnapped and taken out of state by
Confederate raiders who planned to sell them to the
highest bidder. The Carvers offered a reward to get
them back, but only George was rescued. The man who
returned the child to the Carvers was given a horse as
a reward.

From that day on, the Carvers raised George and his
brother, not as slaves but as their own children. George
was a skinny, frail kid, but he had a big brain. He especially loved learning about nature. The local farmers
called him "The Plant Doctor" because he did experiments in a secret garden and figured out how to cure
sick plants.

Although everyone knew he was a genius, George couldn't go to school in his hometown because he was black. More than anything, he wanted to learn—in fact, he dreamed of going to college—so at age twelve, he hit the road looking for an education. George spent years walking across the south. In each new town he searched for a teacher who would take him, stayed until he had learned all he could learn from that person, then moved on, looking for someone who knew more. George slept in barns and basements, washed clothes and did odd jobs to pay his way. All for his brain.

Finally at the age of thirty, George finished enough classes to be accepted into Iowa State College of Agriculture and Mechanic Arts. He was their first and, at that point, only black student. George earned a master's degree in agriculture, and then took a teaching job at the Tuskegee Normal and Industrial Institute in Alabama, one of the only colleges in the country for African Americans. George created their Agricultural Department from scratch, making beakers and chemicals out of junkyard trash!

But George didn't stay put for long. In addition to running the Agriculture Department, teaching classes, and conducting experiments, he built a traveling classroom. He hitched up a horse and wagon and traveled the countryside teaching poor farmers cheaper and easier ways to make their living. On his monthly journeys, he taught southern farmers about "composting"— a cheap and easy way to make crop fertilizer out of dead plants and garbage. He taught them about "crop rotation"—the cotton they were growing sapped nutrients out of the soil in just a few years, so planting other crops, like peanuts, soybeans, and sweet potatoes, was necessary to replace those nutrients. After George's traveling lessons, peanuts, soybeans, and sweet potatoes became three of the most popular and profitable crops in the South.

While teaching at Tuskegee, George became one of the most famous scientists in the world. He thought up over 300 uses for the peanut alone (from peanut shampoo to peanut plastic), along with hundreds of other inventions. Unlike many scientists today, George never earned any money for his discoveries. He believed that he should share his ideas for free. When two of his friends—Henry Ford, inventor of the assembly line and founder of the Ford Motor company, and Thomas Edison, inventor of the electric light—promised George that he'd be rich if he would work with them, he confessed that he had no desire for wealth. If he were to accept money, George told them, he would have to spend time taking care of it and would have less time for inventing and teaching.

It seems that George's unusual childhood journey left a lasting impression: It's your brain that counts.

Chapter 13

Camp Independence

From: Nora E. Coon
Age: 14 years old
Where: U.S.A.

"**D**id you remember your raincoat?" Mom asks.

I roll my eyes. "It's been ninety degrees out for the last two weeks. I do *not* need a raincoat."

"What about some books? Don't spend all your money at the campus bookstore!" Dad smiles as he says it, but I know he's serious.

"Good-*bye*, Dad," I sigh, giving him a hug.

"Don't forget to write! The envelopes are in the—"

"Second pocket from the left in my suitcase. I *know*, Mom. Don't worry, I'll manage!" I hug her also.

There. Just like all the other campers urging their parents
away. Nothing strange. Nothing unusual. Nothing to make me
stand out from the rest.

"Make sure you take your insulin before every meal!" Dad
yells. He's nearly to the car, and I swear the entire camp is
staring at me now.

"And test your blood sugar four times a day!" Mom adds.

Arrgh. I slam the door to my dorm, trying to ignore the
weird looks that I'm getting from other teenagers and *their*
parents.

Alone in my room, I take stock of what I have to survive
on for the next two weeks. Slick-waxed cardboard boxes line
the shelves. One hundred capped needles in sterilized plastic
bags. Four glass tubes of insulin, two cloudy, two clear. Ten fat
black bottles hiding fifty chemically treated strips to measure
my blood sugar: test strips. Thirty soda cans, sticky where
one has leaked, fizzing barely loud enough to be heard. And
three forlorn candy bars, melted out of any recognizable
shape by a three-hour car ride in the July heat.

My summer camp is on the University of Oregon campus
in Eugene, the most liberal pseudo-city in the state. Eugene is
home to most of the underground bands and zines in
Oregon, as well as to stores that if they were anywhere else
wouldn't allow people under twenty-one inside. There's a
Starbucks, a new/used music store, the U of O book/junk
food store, a women's bookstore, a Dairy Queen, and four
shops selling only candy, donuts, Gatorade, and caffeine pills,
all within our camp boundaries. It's the best possible place to
go if you're going to be without your parents for two weeks.

The only contact I have with my parents and the outside

world, the world that can help me with my diabetes, is a crabby cell phone. Covered in blue rubber and with a light-up keypad, bright icons, games, and a half-dead battery, it seems more of a toy than an important technological instrument that can help me manage my illness.

I have strict instructions to stick with my diet—a certain number of carbohydrates at each meal—but as we go to dinner after camp orientation ("Let's see who has the most spirit! On the count of three, yell SPIRIT!"), I realize this will never work. The cafeteria food is stuff that shouldn't be fed to maximum-security prisoners, let alone ninety teenagers starving after three hours without adult supervision. We can eat dinner off-campus if we want, and I'm guessing that Dairy Queen will be getting a lot more business over the next two weeks.

* * * *

A radio alarm goes off—some punk band yelling over electric guitars and drums. Will someone remind me why I'm getting up at 5:30 A.M. during my summer vacation? My arm swings automatically to knock the nuisance away. I have a sudden wonderful image of me smashing the clock until stars and springs fly out of it like they always do in Garfield comics. With a crack, my hand and the alarm clock meet (without any stars, I'm sad to say), and I'm awake. Papers lie scattered across the floor, the result of a frantic search last night that ended a minute after lights-out, when the streetlight outside my window was turned off as well.

I rake the papers together and stuff them into my binder, just as the first harsh lyrics of the heavy-metal wake-up song grate over my ears. Walking down the hall, I hear groans behind closed doors, and as a counselor opens one door, the inhabitant hurls a pillow at her face, shouting, "Change the song!" This is the thirty-seventh time in three days we've heard this song . . . it's getting irritating.

I wash my hair in the bathroom sink—there's a half-hour wait for any of the three showers—and dry it as best I can under the hand dryers. My hair is wild and blown to one side, but it's better than limp and greasy, and I can always beg a brush off someone before classes start. The blood-sugar testing-needle zips in and out of my finger faster than I can see, and a drop of blood beads on the surface. I don't even blink anymore—it's just part of the diabetes. After a year of needles, more than a thousand blood sugar tests and nearly as many shots, a tiny poke is hardly a reason to complain.

I swipe an inch-long test strip across my finger and watch as it sucks the blood in. My blood-testing meter, small enough to fit in the palm of my hand, counts down . . . 5 . . . 4 . . . 3 . . . 2 . . . 1 . . . and then my blood sugar shows. I'm 200, which means there's a little too much sugar in my blood, but it's not really high. My old meter used to take forty-five seconds to count down, and it used so much blood that my fingers were sore whenever I tested.

At 7 A.M., I push and shove and dodge through a crowd of fifty teenagers signing up for special events: Ultimate Frisbee, ice sculpture, botany class, lanyard making, swimming, soccer. Then breakfast: canned orange juice made with too much water, a cinnamon roll so sour my mouth puckers, and a stale donut in a plastic bag for my afternoon snack (in case I don't make it to the campus bookstore).

I give myself an insulin injection, try to ignore the weird

looks people are giving me, realize I don't want to eat all this food, then cram it in my mouth anyway. If I don't eat food after giving myself insulin, I'll get sick, start shaking, and feel faint. Of course, if I eat a cinnamon roll the size of a loaf of bread and drink watered-down orange juice, I may get sick anyway.

I stroll from breakfast, relishing the calm that ignorance brings—my watch has disappeared (I suspect it's under my bed but don't care to look)—until I happen to glance at a clock and dash to my first class, Movie Music. In one of those classrooms that never seems to be warm enough but still makes everyone sleepy, we watch muted video clips on a fuzzy TV, then use keyboards, coat hangers, and cymbals to create movie soundtracks. "Violence as Entertainment" is next. We read through newspapers, magazines, and the Harry Potter books, counting the acts of violence in each. On a fuzzy university TV, we watch Teenage Mutant Ninja Turtles kick, punch, and slapstick their way through half-hour segments of their TV series. By noon I'm so hungry I'm ready to pull a ninja-turtle on anyone who keeps me from getting to lunch.

At lunch, my blood sugar is too low; my legs shake as I walk, and I have to lock my knees to keep from falling. I cut through the lunch line, shrugging off someone's hand as they try to keep me from going ahead of them, and grab my food. Two sodas and a cold piece of pizza later, I'm feeling marginally better.

After lunch, it's two hours of Mock Trial. We look over a fake murder case, complain to the teacher, "If only we had the autopsy . . . ," push the limits of "badgering the witness," and laugh as each side's lawyer imitates his or her favorite

TV attorney. All through my classes, while lawyers-to-be laugh and composers-to-be make music, I surreptitiously test my blood sugar. The needle, the blood, the test strips. The other students watch me: some stare, some glance over, then look away, and others watch me from the corners of their eyes. Why is it no one can resist watching?

My blood sugar is easy to control during classes compared to when I'm doing activities at night. One evening I join in an Ultimate Frisbee game, along with two other girls my age and thirty boys, each at least a head taller than us three girls. My blood sugar begins to plummet the instant I jog out onto the field. I'm tripping over nonexistent things and my hands shake.

Three times during the game my blood sugar dips dangerously. The boys on my team watch, curious, as I stumble to the sidelines and drink soda. Each time I stop, I can't force myself to sit out as long as I should. I get restless, moving from foot to foot, and finally sprint back in and play my hardest. And each time I last about five minutes. Then I'm back on the sidelines, hating diabetes, glaring at anyone who so much as looks at me.

That's not my only close call. Late one night I wake up shaking to find the room spinning around me. My roommate is sprawled comfortably across her bed, her long brown hair tangled over her eyes, one red-nail-polished hand poised to hit the alarm clock. When I turn on a light, she growls and whines at me, "What are you *doing*? It's not five-thirty yet!" But I'm too dizzy to answer her; all I can think about is getting a soda and drinking it so I don't feel like this anymore.

The soda gushes out of the can—another one that's been shaken too much—and onto my desk. My papers float in a puddle of root beer. I swear under my breath and reach for something to mop it up. As I grab a pair of socks, my elbow hits the soda can and it topples to the floor, spraying sticky fizz everywhere. I throw my socks at the mess and open another, not caring when it erupts as well. The soda pours down my throat and I choke on the carbonation.

It takes another soda to get my blood sugar back up, and by then it's 4:30 A.M. I feel much better, but everyone will be getting up in an hour, and I can't fall back asleep. Instead, I lie in bed staring at the ceiling, mentally cursing diabetes with every swear word in my vocabulary.

* * * *

By the time I go home, my diabetes is under control. My parents have called frantically at least five times, but I haven't called them even once. Not to ask for their help, not homesick, not worried. I've had low blood sugars at three in the morning, I've run out of food and had to beg money off friends. I've been through Ultimate Frisbee, nighttime swims, pizza parties, an outdoor market, and two dances. And I've made it. On my own.

I wave to friends as we promise, "We'll e-mail. We'll call. We'll visit each other." We all know that we'll probably never contact one another. Our friendships end with camp—at least until next year. But one thing hasn't ended.

As we drive away, my parents pepper me with questions.

"Were your blood sugars all right?"

"Did you go low often?"

"Did you run out of anything?"

They're still worried about my diabetes. But I'm not. If I survived camp, I can survive anything.

Chapter 14

Sea the World: A Kayaking Experience

From: Jeffrey Shane
Age: 12 years old
Where: Hawaii

Kayaking in the ocean may look easy, but it's not! Last summer, when I traveled to Hawaii with my family, we went on a kayaking trip. Having no previous kayaking experience, we had no clue what we were in for.

The weather was lukewarm and the sky was murky. My parents woke my sister and me up at six in the morning. Not being the adventurous type, I was not at all enthusiastic about the trip. Nevertheless, I gave in, as the alternative would have been to stay at the hotel with some unknown babysitter.

After breakfast, we went to the beach and I got my first glimpse of what a kayak actually is. As I ran to the water, my feet went into shock when they hit the freezing sand. I was surprised. Up until then, I had only felt burning sand, hot from the blistering Hawaiian sun. Obviously, I had never been up this early before.

One of the kayaks was green and the other purple. The kayak body was long, shallow and made of plastic. It hardly seemed seaworthy! In fact, it looked far more suited to a calm lake. Looking out at the swelling ocean waves, I could not imagine how this little, plastic toy boat would manage with me in it!

After what seemed like an eternal lesson from our teacher on how to pilot the kayak (most of which I did not listen to), he finally sent us on our way. I was in the green boat with my dad, while my sister and mom shared the purple boat. When we finally launched into the water, I was thrilled. I thought to myself, "Kayaking isn't so hard after all. In fact, this is actually fun." Within twenty minutes, however, half of my family was fighting. My sister and my mom were struggling to keep up with Dad and me and they were fighting over who was paddling and who was slacking off. Dad and I, on the other hand, were getting along perfectly well. And the scenery was awesome!

A school of ten Spinner dolphins surfaced right next to

our kayak. Spinner dolphins are so named because when they fly up through the air they spin like a top before splashing back down into the water. We watched them play for a while, then headed off to our final destination: Turtle Cove. We planned to anchor our kayaks there and snorkel with the giant sea turtles. By the time we reached Turtle Cove, however, my mother and sister were barely speaking—they had yelled at each other the whole way there. Of course, tying the kayaks together and anchoring them out in the ocean was nowhere near as easy as the teacher had told us it would be. My parents struggled with this task forever. When it was finally done, we jumped into the water, snorkels on, and began searching for turtles.

At first, I felt cheated. I couldn't see any turtles at all. I focused my eyes out on the deeper part of the ocean, straining to view what we had traveled so far to see. Suddenly, I screamed as I felt something nudge my foot. I looked down through the crystal clear water and right below me was a baby sea turtle! He seemed to be as curious about me as I was about him. He swam right up and looked me in the face.

Suddenly, what had been a turtle desert became a turtle island—there were dozens of turtles swimming all around us!

Paddling back to our beach, I was exhausted but happy. And proud of myself. That morning, I had wanted to stay in the hotel room and sleep late. Maybe take a dip in the pool. Instead I discovered a whole new world of beauty and nature. Oh sure, you can see dolphins and turtles on TV all the time, but I got to see them up close in their natural habitat! Dolphins are such beautiful, graceful animals, and turtles are so wise and curious—I hate to think about how we take advantage of them.

After kayaking Hawaii, I have a totally different view of Sea World. Now it seems sad that all those intelligent animals have to live in captivity, performing for humans. I'm sure they'd rather be out in the ocean, playing with the occasional kayaker. I am not sure that I ever want to go kayaking again with my family, but it definitely was an experience that I never want to forget. I saw the world through the sea.

Dana Starkell

b. 1961 – ✦ From Canada to the Amazon

Does the thought of being stuck on a weeklong car trip with your parents terrify you? The claustrophobic space . . . the monotonous scenery . . . the ridiculous singing? Imagine then, being trapped in a tiny canoe, alone with your dad for two whole years! And yet Dana Starkell survived 730 days in a twenty-one-foot canoe, as he and his father paddled from their home in Winnipeg, Canada, to the mouth of the Amazon River. In the course of their marathon adventure, Dana not only braved some serious "alone time" with Dad but also raging rapids, monster waves, murderous locals, and more biting insects than you can possibly imagine.

It was June 1, 1980, when nineteen-year-old Dana, his older brother, Jeff, and their dad, Don, packed up their canoe and launched into the Red River in Canada. They had been planning the trip for years—a kind of father-son bonding journey. The three of them bonded all the way through Canada and then down the mighty Mississippi River, alongside the grand paddleboats. Then they bonded some more as they snaked through the bayous of Louisiana, amongst the crocodiles and water moccasins.

But when they hit the terrifying waters of the Gulf of Mexico, the bonding was over. Giant waves and blasting winds capsized their canoe countless times. After weeks of near-death experiences at sea, Jeff called it quits in Veracruz, Mexico. He told his little brother, "It's just too crazy out there! It's suicide!" and flew home.

Dana and his dad were on their own. They continued their suicidal mission, paddling along the eastern shore of Mexico, north over the Yucatan Peninsula, and then south again into Central America, where a variety of wars and revolutions were underway. After surviving a hurricane on a tiny, unprotected island in Belize, they were nearly murdered by drunken thieves in Honduras and revolutionary soldiers in Nicaragua, who mistook them for American spies. No one believed that these two Robinson Crusoe–looking guys really could have paddled all the way down from Canada—thousands of miles away.

After narrowly escaping with their lives, Dana and his father tried to canoe through the famous Panama Canal but were denied passage. The reason? Authorities claimed their canoe was "not seaworthy"—after more than five months at sea!

If Dana thought Central America was tough, the waters of South America made it look like a paddle in the park. From the moment they hit Colombia, pirates and paranoid drug smugglers attacked their canoe almost daily. All they had to protect themselves with was a machete and their own funky odor (not too many showers on that canoe)! They not only fought off the attackers, but they also encountered a surprising amount of kindness. When they ran out of food and were starving along a deserted stretch of Venezuelan coast, the Guajira Indians came to their rescue. And at the end of the ocean portion of their journey, they celebrated a cheerful Christmas among the Rastafarians of Trinidad.

The final leg of their trip was along the rivers of the Amazon rainforest. Their last four months were filled with pink river dolphins, howler monkeys, sloths, capybaras, parrots, crocodiles, piranhas, anacondas, and countless other birds, animals, and insects. And did I mention mosquitoes? Dana, who loves nature, was in heaven. Although he nearly died of food poisoning and once had to eat a dinner full of maggots, this was his favorite part of the journey.

Sunburned and covered with bug bites, they finally made it to the end of their journey: the *boca* (mouth) of the Amazon River. In those two years, Dana had literally millions of strokes with his paddle. He had slept in Indian shacks, on sandbars, in the jungle, and sometimes in the floating canoe. He had survived by eating whatever was available: shark, turtle, tapir, cactus, and even roasted ants! He had remained calm when the canoe capsized and broke apart on rocks or coral—an amazing forty-five times! And yet, with his own strength (and his dad's), Dana made it well over 12,000 miles—more than half the distance around the world—and into the Guinness Book of World Records for the longest canoe journey ever made.

Although much of the trip was pretty grim (not to mention dangerous), Dana reveled in the adventure. The asthma that plagued him as a child disappeared forever. And his two great loves—the guitar and nature—got plenty of attention. His trip showed him both the good and the bad sides of Mother Nature: her miracles and her mighty strength. And he had so much time to practice playing guitar on deserted stretches of beach that he's now a professional musician in Canada.

Chapter 15

View from the Top and the Bottom

From: Alice Shteyn
Age: 13 years old
Where: Canada

The week before my family's winter vacation was a chaotic madhouse. While my parents rented skis and an apartment in Canada's Big White Resort and my brother ran around the house like a frenzied dog trying to find a bone, I was frantically trying on every sweater that existed in my closet and going on archaeological excavations to find long-lost mittens.

But I knew the constant banging into each other and fighting over snow pants would all be worth it. It was going to be the perfect break—snow, skiing, and hot chocolate

every day! I could almost taste the crisp, cool air of the gleaming Canadian Rockies already!

When the day of departure finally came, I felt like a giddy puppy going to my first show. I didn't mind that people stepped on my toes at the airport or that the check-in line was a mile long. I didn't even mind that we would be flying for at least four hours before we could even feel the crunchy, white powder beneath our feet.

On the plane I acted like any other kid: "Are we there yet? How much longer? I need to go to the bathroom." I had too much pent-up energy inside me and I was ready to play. Finally after hours in the air, another hour of hectic baggage claim *and* car rental, we made the two-hour drive to our final destination. It was two in the morning when we arrived at our apartment, but finally it was time for the fun to begin!

The mountains were every bit as perfect as I'd imagined. The glistening pinnacle of Big White Mountain shone in the moonlight, and I had no doubts that it would look even better in the frosty sunshine the next day. I was right.

Glittering snow winked at me from my perch on the shimmering peak. Mom stood next to me, smiling with a sparkle of excitement in her eye. We were in for the thrill of a lifetime—skiing on one of the biggest mountains in North America! I grasped my lemon-colored ski poles tightly and readjusted my matching beanie.

"Ready?" I asked my mom.

"Ready when you are," she replied.

Together, we pushed off and began whizzing down the mountain, light and elated, like a pair of helium-filled balloons.

"I feel so free!" I shouted.

"Me, too!" Mom laughed. "It feels like nothing matters... just getting to the bottom!"

Only, my mom didn't get to the bottom.

Freeze that image. Standing on the mountaintop, I felt so carefree; I had the wind in my hair, a free spirit in my soul, and energy pulsing down to my boots. I was a kid flying down a sparkling silver snow slide—I had no idea that when I reached the bottom, I would no longer be the same kid. The bottom ... Though I didn't realize it then, at the bottom of the mountain my life was going to change.

When I got to the end of the run, I waited for my mom at the chair lift, flexing my fingers to keep warm. I must have passed her on the way down, I thought. She'll be here soon. I could picture her skiing down, maybe with some snow in her flyaway hair and her cheeks pink from the cold.

I waited for five minutes. Then ten ... twenty ... thirty.

She didn't ski down. Maybe she was waiting for me at the top, looking for me to get off the chair. I made my way back up, scanning the snow below for my mom's cheery grin and her sky-blue ski pants. At the top of the lift, I searched the area. Not a ski pole in sight. By this time I was getting worried, but I figured I'd meet her at the end of the day and we'd laugh about our silly skiing and losing each other. Besides, we would probably bump into each other sometime during the day. I mean, there are only so many green runs for beginners like us!

The rest of the day passed in a flash: up the chair lift, down the mountain, shake, shake, shake the snow off the boots and up the lift again. Although I was having fun, I was eager to get back to the apartment and find out where my mom had been the whole day.

As the clock tower in the little ski village struck four, I hurried up the stairs to our home away from home. In a quick jingle of keys, the door swished open and I looked around, disappointment settling in my stomach. No one was home.

Oh well, I thought, they'll turn up. Within an hour my dad and my older brother returned, bursting in with ecstatic grins. My mom did not.

Instead, we opened the door to a somber-looking ski patrol guy in a red and white uniform. He looked at us grimly.

"Your mother is in the hospital. She's had a serious accident."

Mom had lost control of her skis and crashed into a tree. She had broken her arm and four ribs and dislocated her shoulder. While I was oblivious at the bottom of the ski run, the ski patrol had loaded her onto a snow stretcher and zoomed down the mountain to a waiting ambulance. She was at a hospital in Kelowna, B.C., two hours away, waiting to have surgery the next morning. Ski Patrol man told us she was lucky it wasn't worse.

After those words, I couldn't see, I couldn't hear, I couldn't even think. It was like a creeping white fog covering a path so you don't know what's going on or what's up ahead, but somehow you still have to press on. The fog bearing the terrible news enveloped my mind.

After the surgery, Mom came back with her arm in a huge sling and bandages covering her torso completely. When I saw her, I almost burst into tears.

"How are you feeling?" I asked.

"I'm okay, kitty. Don't worry about me," she answered, but I couldn't help noticing her staggered breathing because of the pain in her ribs—and everywhere else.

Mom wanted the rest of us to have fun on our vacation, so we tried to keep going. But believe it or not, the next day my dad pulled a muscle in his back while cross-country skiing, and he was out for the rest of the trip.

Our parents' slogan became: "Life goes on." They told my brother and me to enjoy ourselves on the slopes and to tell them about our adventures each day. And so we did. We worked hard at ski school and tried to keep up the spirit of our now small team. But when I skied down the same slopes as that first day, I knew something inside me had changed.

Now you're probably thinking: "Okay, that was some bad luck, but at least the kids got to have some fun." I wish. More bad luck was headed our way.

Not two days later, my brother got hit in the face by a wayward T-bar. It was like déjà vu. He was rushed to the ambulance by ski patrol and then off to the hospital. The same Ski Patrol man stood in our doorway once again and told us the grim prognosis:

"Broken teeth, broken jaw."

By now I was thinking, "Why us? What did we ever do to deserve this?" My parents were beside themselves. We realized then that our luck was up. The mountain had beaten us. We packed up our gear and rushed home so my brother could have his surgery in the U.S.

Back home, thirteen-year-old me became the anchor of the family. I was the only person in one piece, and I held us together. I organized Mom's medications, made tea for my dad, and made oatmeal for my brother's breakfast. I cheered them up and reminded everyone, "Be grateful that we're still together." They tried to smile.

For months now, I have been learning what responsibility really is. Since we returned from our very unlucky vacation, my mom hasn't been able to go back to her job as a nurse. She's had three surgeries, numerous infections, and a tube in her arm to pump antibiotics into her veins. My dad has had trouble with his job as well. His research lab group was mostly laid off, but he was lucky just to switch offices and keep some sort of job. And he still has back pain.

My brother recovered pretty quickly, but he couldn't stand drinking all his meals while his jaw healed. He drank milk shakes, smoothies, and pureed mashed potatoes (yummy—not!) for three months. Everything had to go through the blender before it could go on his plate (or should I say, in his cup).

As for me, daily chores that Mom used to do await me every morning and evening when I'm not in school. Although you might think I resent doing the laundry, vacuuming the house, and making the meals, I know my family is grateful every time I ask how they're feeling . . . while I'm loading the dishwasher.

When I skied down that freshly powdered mountain in Canada, a transformation took place. At the top of the mountain, I believed that my mom, my dad, and my older brother would always be there to take care of me. They would always make my lunches, drive me to school when it's raining, compliment me on my gymnastics routine, or clap for me at a piano recital.

But after spending some time at the bottom of the mountain, I feel older, more mature, and capable of handling whatever bad luck life throws my way. I was plunged into the icy reality of life. It was my turn to be there for my family and to learn how to be independent, brave, and strong for them. The views from the top and bottom are certainly not the same, but I'm learning to handle the differences.

Chapter 16

Zai Jian Hong Kong, Hello Oregon

From: Marshall Frimoth
Age: 10 years old
Where: Hong Kong
& the U.S.A.

Hong Kong was my home. Although I was born in Portland, Oregon, and visited there every summer, I lived on a beautiful island from the time I was three years old. For five years I was used to hearing Mandarin spoken in the streets, walking to the market beneath huge, immense buildings, and eating *dim sum* for dinner.

Then one summer, during our annual vacation in Oregon, my mom asked me, "Do you like it here in Portland?"

"Yeah," I said. "It's pretty cool."

"Would you like to live here?"

"You mean leave behind all my friends in Hong Kong?" I asked. "No way!"

Somewhere in the back of my mind, I knew that my parents were considering moving back to Oregon, but I managed to avoid thinking about it again, until the next winter back in Hong Kong, that is. That's when the bomb dropped.

"Your father and I have something to tell you," Mom said just before dinner one night. "Next summer our family is moving back to Portland."

I was so shocked I dropped the forks I was setting on the table. How could I leave behind all my good friends? And what about the other things I'd miss if we left Hong Kong, things I grew up with that I'd never see again? Like the smell of incense burning in the temples and the huge double-decker buses that tilt like the Leaning Tower of Pisa when they turn on narrow Hong Kong streets? I loved sitting by the top windows of the bus, looking down at everyone strolling below. And what about the Mid-Autumn Festival, when everyone goes to the beach on a full-moon night, lights candles, and sticks them in the sand? Oregon could never replace Hong Kong.

Seven depressing months later, the packing company came. It took them a week to box up all our belongings and ship them to the States. At the end of that long week, it was time to go. After saying our good-byes, I had to take one last look at our flat. I felt strange standing in our empty home, seeing where my bed, dresser, and other things used to be. The floor-to-ceiling windows all around the flat made me feel like I was standing in a fishbowl. I had always loved gazing out them and seeing the Mt. Parker Observatory flashing its little red light at me. Now the echo of the empty flat felt like it had when we moved in five years before.

A little red taxi was waiting outside. My family and I struggled to cram our many suitcases, backpacks, and boxes into the cab in the sweltering heat of the Hong Kong summer. The taxi ride was long, hot, tiring, and extremely uncomfortable with all the luggage on every side of me, squishing me flat as a Hong Kong dollar.

After thirty minutes of getting bonked around in the taxi, we arrived at the newly constructed, mammoth Chep Lap Kok International Airport. Sounds of foreign languages filled my ears as I walked into a terminal big enough to be Godzilla's bedroom.

Waiting in line to get on the plane, I knew what was coming: fifteen hours of sitting down, doing nothing, and feeling like I was watching a tree grow. What would happen *after* the plane ride was harder to imagine. I would have to adjust to a new life. A new life of not knowing anyone . . . in a place far, far away. As we touched down in Portland, I was relieved that the ride, and the worrying, was over.

Just seeing the tiny Portland airport, I felt overwhelmed. I wanted to run back home, to my better life in Hong Kong. But as soon as I stepped off the plane, I knew it was too late: I had

arrived at the place I dreaded.
Then, all of a sudden, I was surrounded by people I knew. All
of my grandparents, uncles,
aunts, and cousins were at the
gate to welcome us. I was
immediately surrounded by
hugs and kisses and smiles.
Their love surrounded me, but I
was still a little uncomfortable
with being away from my home
in Hong Kong.

My first day of school in
America, I was sweating with
nervousness. I expected to see
a bunch of different cultures, like in Hong Kong. I was used to
hanging out with Korean, Chinese, and Indian kids at my old
international school. Instead, my school was full of mostly
American kids doing American things. I had to get used to
this new American world. Kids use different slang words—
everyone here says "yup" instead of "yes" and "hey" instead
of "hello." And in America, kids play football instead of the
rugby I love. People here also drive gigantic SUVs, where in
Hong Kong we used buses, taxis, subways, and *tiny* cars. It's
very weird here!

Now that I've been back for two years, I've gotten used
to the differences and made tons of new friends. I realize
now that there are more cultures here than I had thought at
the start. In our neighborhood we've got Chinese, Romanian,
Korean, and Fijian families living on every corner. I used to

love climbing the crooked trees at the Hong Kong beaches, but now sliding down the dunes on the Oregon coast is just as fun. Sitting on the top level of the double-decker buses used to make me feel like I was going to crash into a tree, but the super-fast MAX train in Portland that zooms all around town gives me the same thrill.

I still miss Hong Kong a lot, but now I'm learning about life in Oregon, and its becoming my new home. The ancient Chinese philosopher Confucius once said, "Learn eagerly and cherish your knowledge as not to lose it." What I learned in Hong Kong will always be in my heart and will never be forgotten.

Marco Polo
1254 – 1324 ✦ From Italy to China

Have you ever played the game "Marco Polo" in a swimming pool? (One person closes her eyes and yells
"Marco," while the other players scream "Polo" and
race around trying not to get tagged by her.) Did you
ever stop and wonder who Mr. Polo was? Some blind
lunatic who attacked innocent swimmers? Actually, no.
He was one of the most famous travelers of all time. He
didn't just cross a swimming pool—as a teenager, Polo
crossed thousands of miles of uncharted oceans and
dangerous lands on one of the greatest journeys
of all time.

It all started back in Venice, Italy, where Marco's
father was a merchant. Shortly after Marco was born,
his father took off on a long trading trip. So long, in
fact, that he was absent for most of Marco's childhood.
While his father was away, Marco's mother died. Marco
was not a lucky guy.

When Marco was fifteen, however, his luck changed.
His father and uncle returned to Venice, boasting of
treasures in the East. They had been all the way to
China and back! In those days, without planes, trains
and automobiles, a trip of that kind was almost unheard
of—European travelers who tried it were likely to be
killed by bandits or by people who hated foreigners. But
there was a new ruler in China, Kublai Khan, and he

wanted to meet these strange Europeans he had heard about. He made the roads through Asia safer so that Europeans could come to his land. The Polos were the first Europeans Khan had ever met. He asked them to go back to Europe and return with 100 Christian missionaries and some holy oil from Jerusalem, both of which he thought would give him magical powers. In exchange he would make the brothers wealthy beyond their wildest dreams.

So they were back in Venice, preparing to repeat their dangerous journey. Marco begged to go along, but his father said that he was too young. Fortunately it took the men two years to prepare, and by the time they were ready to leave, Marco's father realized that his seventeen-year-old son would be a great help on the expedition. Marco could go.

In 1271 Marco, his father, and his uncle set out on their great adventure. They brought oil as a gift from the Pope, but the missionaries were too afraid to go to China. Christians were not exactly popular outside of Europe. Khan would have to be satisfied with the holy oil. The Polos traveled thousands of miles, walking the Spice Road through Persia, riding camels through the deserts of Arabia, and climbing the mountain passes of Asia, and all the while Marco kept a journal about the amazing things he saw. After three years on the road, Marco finally reached China!

When the great Khan first met Marco, he was impressed with the young man's honesty and story-telling abilities. He asked Marco to work for him, traveling his vast empire and reporting back on what was going on. It was a dangerous job—Marco had to watch out for Khan's enemies, not to mention wild animals— but he was itching for more adventure.

Although Khan did not want them to leave, the Polos had gotten what they came for. They had made their fortune and were eager to get home. But how would they haul their booty through bandit-filled lands? Chinese paper money was worthless in Europe and gold was too heavy to carry, so the Polos traded their riches for diamonds, rubies, emeralds, sapphires, and pearls. They ripped open the seams of their clothes and sewed the gems inside. No one could tell that they carried riches inside their tattered traveling clothes!

When Marco once again caught sight of the churches and canals of Venice, he had been away from home for 24 years! At first, no one believed Marco's outrageous tales. But eventually, they were persuaded. How else could he have gotten so rich? A few years after their return, Venice went to war and Marco was captured while commanding a battleship. His bad luck was back and he was thrown into jail.

Prison was not the most exciting place, so Marco, with his wild travel stories, became the most popular guy around. With plenty of time to kill, Marco wrote his stories down in a book, which became a medieval bestseller! Soon, everyone in Europe knew of Marco and his adventure. When he got out of prison, he was famous!

After Kublai Khan died, the land route to Asia became impassable once again. Europeans were unable to go that way for decades, and Marco's stories became legends. Even after his death, his book lived on. Mapmakers and explorers used it. And 175 years after Marco wrote it, Christopher Columbus had a copy of the book on board his ship when he "discovered" America. Since the land route to Asia that Marco described was closed, Columbus was searching for a way by sea when he accidentally stumbled upon a new world. Who knows? Without Marco Polo to inspire him, Columbus might never have left Italy. And without Marco Polo, what game would we play in the pool today?

Chapter 17

On My Own Road

From: Sarah Stillman
Age: 19 years old
Where: Cuba

I am nothing like Jack Kerouac. I've never hitchhiked or fallen in love with a dark, mysterious stranger. I've never scribbled drunken poetry or watched the sunset in all its San Francisco grandeur from the back of a moving freight train. So when my best friend gave me a birthday gift of Kerouac's renowned book, *On the Road*, I felt justified in my temptation to disregard it. How could I possibly relate to a story about three crazy travelers and their opium-laced escapades? In school, I'd learned that Kerouac was a sexist, homophobic nutcase. Apparently, his journeys danced a razor-thin edge

143

between reverence for life and self-destructive hedonism. Nevertheless, before departing for Cuba in July 2000 I tossed my fresh-smelling copy of *On the Road* into my suitcase. From that moment on, despite how much I tried to resist, Jack Kerouac seized a firm grip upon my imagination and taught me what it means to travel with a free spirit.

I turned to the first page of *On the Road* while seated in a strange Cancun hotel room, crying. About two hours earlier, I'd gotten off a plane, ready for a one-night layover before reaching my final destination—Havana. I was en route to spending two weeks of my summer vacation in the capital of Cuba, doing volunteer work for an organization called the International Outreach Center and perfecting my Spanish. Very few Americans are allowed into communist Cuba each year, due to the economic embargo, so I was already expecting a few difficulties on the journey ahead. Still, I had no idea how quickly my troubles would come; the moment I hailed a cab from the airport in Cancun, chaos ensued. After speaking in mangled Spanish with my cab driver, I discovered that my dad had accidentally booked me into the wrong hotel, some 100 miles away from the airport. In other words, I was all by myself for the first time in a foreign country, with nowhere to sleep, no one to talk to, and no idea what to do.

At first, I panicked. My face grew bright red and I forgot every Spanish word I ever knew. I wanted to cry, scream, or run towards home as fast as I could. I eventually remembered how to ask the cab driver to take me downtown, which he did. There, I found a pay phone and tried to call home—no answer.

Across the street, I spotted the flimsy green awning of a

hotel and decided to take a chance on it. I entered the brick building, approached the front desk, and explained my dilemma to the manager, who turned out to be an incredibly kind man with a daughter my age. He booked me into a room on the second floor, where I finally sat down to rest—with my chair propped against the door to compensate for the broken lock. My heart was still beating triple-speed, but the tension in my shoulders slowly released. I let myself cry a few quick tears before trying to divert my attention from my anxiety and isolation. Then, not knowing what else to do, I took out my book and started to read.

With brilliance and lyricism, Kerouac managed to transform my state of mind. In chapter one, he convinced me that the best travelers *thrive* on chaos. I listened intently as the main character, Sal, proclaimed:

> *The only people for me are the mad ones, the ones who are mad to live, mad to talk, mad to be saved, desirous of every thing at the same time, the ones who never yawn or say a commonplace thing, but burn, burn, burn like fabulous yellow roman candles . . .*

Something inside me stirred. *I* wanted to be mad to live, mad to experience everything the world would toss at me. I didn't want to shy away from the new smells of the city street, the sound of the vendors selling ripe mangos, and all the other sensations of the Mexican night. Why should I let my hellish day evolve into an equally hellish night, thus robbing me of a chance to see Cancun beyond my dusty hotel window? Boldly, I tossed down my book, stuffed some *pesos* into my pocket, and went out to find myself a warm tortilla and a cozy spot to people-watch. As I emerged into the humid summer air, I felt that a wall within me had fallen and somehow, I realized I had become Jack Kerouac's disciple— on the road and loving it.

My surreal night in Cancun was only a brief introduction to the merits of Kerouac's "go with the flow" approach to travel. When I reached Havana the next day, I remembered that my journey was just officially beginning and that I had two more weeks of fertile practice ground on which to try out my new philosophy of spontaneity; I would be living in a Cuban family's apartment and working in a human rights library each afternoon. On my first night, I learned how to sleep in a boiling hot room with no fan or air conditioner (but plenty of mosquitoes eager to turn my legs and arms into a feasting ground).

The second night, I learned how to remain calm while looking for the hundred-dollar bill I'd lost (my main stash of money for the trip, which my mom had brilliantly convinced me to hide inside an empty tampon applicator, for "safekeeping"). Almost every hour I spent in Cuba had its unique anxieties, and that's what I often loved about it, oddly enough; each problem that tumbled my way was another exercise in flexibility, forcing me to stay on my toes and cope creatively.

Back at home, I was a compulsive seeker of predictability, always trying to ensure that my schoolwork was in perfect order, that my parents and friends felt just the way I wanted them to, and that my emotions stayed out of uncertain or ambiguous "gray spaces." In Cuba, such comforts were no longer an option. I had little choice but to embrace the blistering heat, lost items, language barrier, and even a small case of food poisoning as a part of the grand adventure.

Of course, my thrills weren't exclusively derived from miseries, and I don't mean to imply that good travelers must also be masochists. The most dazzling moments of my trip were often quite luxurious—licking an ice cream cone while gazing upon a breathtaking Cuban sunset, for example. Reflecting on my experiences through the lens of Kerouac's philosophy, I can see that the highlights generally came from a willingness to endure discomfort in exchange for the wonders Cuba had to offer. I'm not a courageous person, but Kerouac coaxed me into doing things I normally wouldn't dare to, such as dancing wildly in the middle of a circle of Cubans during a holiday festival. Some of the most memorable risks I took may seem like the smallest ones. Because I was staying with a Cuban family and two American college students, I truly had to come out of my shell, get to know my hosts and fellow Americans, and form bonds with each of them. Learning to develop close human relationships with total strangers, especially across cultural and generational divides, is probably the best lesson I've kept with me since Cuba.

That magical summer of reading, living, and breathing *On the Road* was my first encounter with the transformative power of traveling, but thankfully not my last. Since then, I've held hands with a chimpanzee in a Bangkok zoo, bargained for strange fruits in a Mexican marketplace, watched a game of nude basketball in a Copenhagen park, and interviewed young women workers at a Barbie factory in Asia. I feel incredibly grateful for these opportunities and also for

Kerouac's guidance in being open to them. He's helped me to see how much is lost when we fear chaos, stick to a rigid plan, and shut ourselves off to the world of infinite joys and sorrows.

This lesson goes far beyond just traveling; the beatnik spirit of acceptance and fearlessness can make all the difference between a frustrated life and a celebratory one. I think Kerouac said it best with the mantra that made him the hero of the 1950s Beat generation and, five decades later, of a sixteen-year-old girl alone in a Cancun hotel room: "I just go along. I dig life."

Travel Resources

Now that you've read about some of the adventures enjoyed by kids all over the world, you're probably curious about different kinds of travel opportunities. If you're interested in exciting journeys and ready to do a little research, this list of travel resources should be helpful. Have fun planning your great adventure!

General Travel

www.familytravelforum.com
Contains an index of family-travel links and family-centered travel agents.

www.fodors.com
Offers lots of travel information on almost any country in the world. Also has a service to help you translate important phrases before you travel.

www.gapyear.com
Provides links and advice toward travel that help young adults discover themselves and to establish a sense of their own identity.

www.istc.umn.edu
International Service and Travel Center offers a searchable database of travel programs. The site also offers a lot of helpful advice about travel preparation.

www.kidtravels.com
Provides information and links to travel opportunities for kids and families.

www.lonelyplanet.com
Provides travelers with reliable, comprehensive, and independent travel information.

www.nols.edu
National Outdoor Leadership School offers courses lasting 10 days to a full semester, taught in beautiful wilderness locations.

www.travelforkids.com
Lists fun activities and great places to eat all around the world. Many other travel tips, too!

Youth Camps

www.kidscamps.com
Provides a listing of all kinds of summer camps in the United States, as well as some travel opportunities abroad.

www.outwardbound.com
Outward Bound USA offers information on adventure education for youths and adults.

www.paliadventures.com
Pali Overnight Adventures has a variety of overnight camp programs for kids and teens.

Study Abroad/Volunteer Abroad

www.afs.org
American Field Service is a volunteer organization that provides student exchange opportunities for high-school age students. They offer placement in over 70 countries.

www.coolworks.com/vlnteer.htm
Contains a list of teen jobs and volunteer programs found across the United States and abroad.

www.i-to-i.com
Contains information on volunteer opportunities for those 17 to 70 to work and teach around the world.

www.idealist.org/kt/index.html
Contains information about youth volunteer programs.

www.planetedu.com
Lists opportunities for study abroad, overseas language programs, and volunteer positions.

www.studentambassadors.org
The People to People Student Ambassador Program provides

overseas experience for middle school and high school students.

www.studyabroad.com
Provides listings of international work, internship, and volunteer programs.

www.usexperiment.org
Experiment in International Living offers study abroad summer programs for high school students. Each program immerses participants in the daily life of another culture.

www.volunteerabroad.com
Lists extensive information about high school volunteer programs available world wide.

Other Books by Beyond Words

EVER IMAGINE CREATING YOUR OWN COMIC BOOKS?
Why just imagine? Make it happen!
Get great tips on:

- Starting a studio and choosing the right tools

- Creating your own characters and stories

- Developing your drawing techniques

- Submitting and selling your comics

Written by the editor of Dark Horse Comics, Phil Amara, with advice from other comic book professionals and kids who are currently getting their work noticed, *So, You Wanna Be a Comic Book Artist?* will tell you how to turn your love of comic books into a career. It doesn't matter if you're just beginning or have been drawing your own comics for years. ANYONE can create their own comic books—let your imagination soar!

144 pages, black and white art, $9.95 softcover

IS THERE A ROCK STAR IN THE HOUSE?
It could be you! All you budding musicologists, get the scoop on:

- Choosing the perfect name for your band

- Finding song ideas

- Creating a demo tape

✳ Scholastic & Book of the Month Club Selection ✳

How did Britney Spears get her start? This book won't tell you that, but it will inspire you to live your rock and roll dream: from how to start a band, to how to get discovered, and everything in between (like finding the perfect look and attitude to express your musical soul, and, of course, getting your parents on board to the whole idea of you as a rock star).

152 pages, black and white art, $8.95 softcover

HEY BOYS! WHY WAIT FOR SUCCESS?

Did you know:

- Galileo invented the first accurate mechanical clock at the age eighteen?

- Louis Braille created an alphabet system for the blind when he was only fifteen?

- Bill Gates founded his first computer company and invented a machine to solve traffic problems at sixteen?

Boys Who Rocked the World shares the stories of boys who have made a difference in the world before the age of twenty and also profiles boys currently preparing to take the world by storm. Now it's your turn! The world is waiting to be rocked!

160 pages, black and white art, $8.95 softcover

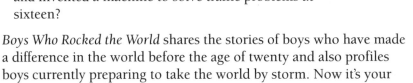

GREAT STORIES OF REAL GIRLS WHO MADE HISTORY!

Did you know that:

- Joan of Arc was only 17 when she led the French troops to victory?

- Cristen Powell started drag racing at 16 and is now one of the top drag racers in America?

- Wang Yani began painting at the age of three? She was the youngest artist ever to have her own exhibit at the Smithsonian museum!

✳ Scholastic & Book of the Month Club Selection ✳

Impress your girlfriends with even more great stories of women heroines with *Girls Who Rocked the World 2*.

✳ A Troll Book Club Selection ✳

So . . . how are you going to rock the world?

160 pages, black and white illustrations, $8.95 softcover

DO YOU KNOW THE REAL YOU?

Everywhere you turn, teen magazines are telling you how to look and who you're supposed to be. Shouldn't YOU be the authority on yourself? Sixteen-year-old Sarah Stillman offers an escape from superficiality in her book *Soul Searching: A Girl's Guide to Finding Herself.* Learn how to:

- Create a calming atmosphere for yourself through Feng Shui and Aromatherapy
- Relax with yoga and meditation
- Keep a journal and analyze your dreams
- Find your passions and accomplish your goals

It's time to start discovering yourself—you never know what you might find!

140 pages, black and white art, $10.95 softcover

DOES YOUR MEOWER HAVE PSYCHIC POWER?
DOES FIDO KNOW THINGS YOU DON'T KNOW?

Do you dare to explore the uncharted world of your pet's brain? Read about:

- Spooky stories of pets with psychic powers
- Tests to find out if your pet is psychic
- Ways to increase your pet's psychic abilities
- Astrology charts for your pet

✳ Scholastic & Book of the Month Club Selection ✳

Can your cat get out of the house even when all the doors are closed? Has your dog ever seen a ghost? Does your horse seem to read your mind? If you can answer yes to any of these questions, you might have (are you sitting down?) a psychic pet! Better keep that food dish filled from now on!

124 pages, black and white art, $7.95 softcover

KIDSMAKINGMONEY.COM

Okay, *Better Than a Lemonade Stand,* by fifteen-year-old author Daryl Bernstein, is not a guide to high tech riches. But computers aren't the only way to get rich quick. Daryl started his first business when he was only eight! Since then, he has tried all fifty-one of the kid businesses in this book, all of which are easy to start up. Today, Daryl runs his own multimillion-dollar business and is happy to share with you the secrets of his success.

Learn how you can earn bucks by being a:
- baby-sitting broker

- dog walker

- mural painter and many, many more fun money making jobs!!!

✳ A Doubleday Book Club Selection ✳

150 pages, black and white cartoon illustrations, $9.95 softcover

EXCUSES! EXCUSES!

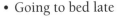

Authors Mike and Zach are excuse experts. These nine- and ten-year-old best friends have created *100 Excuses for Kids,* a hysterical book which will give you great excuses for getting out of anything—vegetables, homework, chores whatever! Get the latest and newest excuses for:
- Going to bed late

- Not eating your vegetables

- Not cleaning your room and many (97 to be exact), many more!

✳ Scholastic Book Club Selection ✳

96 pages, black and white cartoon art, $5.95 softcover

HEY, GIRLS!
SPEAK OUT • BE HEARD• BE CREATIVE • GO FOR YOUR DREAMS!

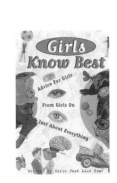

Discover how you can:
- handle grouchy, just plain ornery adults

- pass notes in class without getting caught

•

• avoid life's most embarrassing moments

✳ Scholastic & Book of the Month Club Selection ✳

Girls Know Best celebrates girls' unique voices and wisdom. 38 girls, ages 7-15, share their advice and activities. Everything you need to know . . . from the people who've been there: girls just like you!

160 pages, black and white collage art, $8.95 softcover

LISTEN UP!
GIRLS HAVE MORE TO SAY!
More girl wisdom on:
• how to have the best slumber party ever

• discovering the meanings of your dreams

• overcoming any obstacle, whenever, wherever

160 pages, black and white collage art, $8.95 softcover

GIRLS CANNOT BE SILENCED!
EVEN MORE GIRL TALK!
Answers all your questions about:
• different religions

• starting your own rock band

• whether alternative schooling is for you and, of course, much, much more!

132 pages, black and white collage art, $8.95 softcover

HEY, GUYS!
EVERYTHING YOU NEED TO KNOW, ACCORDING TO THE "EXPERTS"—GUYS JUST LIKE YOU!
Read about:
• tips on catching frogs, bugs, and other creatures

• wise-cracks to make your buddies laugh

- being the best big brother

- the scoop on girls

From making comic strips to dealing with girls, *Boys Know It All* is packed with great ideas from thirty-two cool guys —just like you!

160 pages, black and white collage art, $8.95 softcover

GROWING UP JUST GOT A LITTLE EASIER

Life can be tough, especially when you're in between everything. *The Girls Life Guide to Growing Up* helps relieve the stress of "tweendom" and "teendom" and shows you how to deal with:
- She's All That—Or is She? The myths of hangin' with the "in" crowd are busted by girls who have been there.

- What Kind of Smart Are You? Intelligence is more than a grade on a math test. This quiz reveals your true talents.

- Whose Body Is This, Anyway? Yeah, you're going through some crazy changes. Know what to expect and how to cope.

❋ Scholastic Book Club Selection ❋

It's as cool an advice book as you'll ever want, written by the staff of your favorite magazine, Girls Life. Take the quizzes, read the chapters and become self aware! See what guys really think about all this girl stuff, and laugh out loud as you read about everything girl, from friends, family, crushes, school, your body, and most of all, you!

272 pages, black and white illustrations, $11.95 softcover

TO ORDER ANY OF THE BOOKS LISTED HERE OR TO REQUEST A CATALOG, PLEASE CONTACT US OR MAIL US THIS ORDER FORM.

Name _____

Address _____

City _____ State/Province_____ Zip/Postal Code _____

Country _____

Phone Number _____

Title	Quantity	Price	Line Total

Subtotal _____

Shipping (see below) _____

Total _____

We accept Visa, MasterCard, and American Express, or send a check or money order payable to Beyond Words Publishing.

Credit Card Number _____ Exp. Date _____

Shipping Rates (within the United States only)
First book: $3.00   Each additional book: $1.00
Please call for special shipping services (overnight or international).

Beyond Words Publishing, Inc.
20827 NW Cornell Road, Suite 500
Hillsboro, OR 97124-9808

or contact us by phone:
(503) 531-8700
fax: (503) 531-8773
email: sales@beyondword.com